Reece in Pieces

Nataisha T. Hill

Published by TaiLorMade Books

Chapter 1

Reece was getting restless as she sat outside on the concrete steps of their overcrowded apartment complex. It seemed like every family in the building had six kids, three uncles, two aunts, seven cousins, and two dogs under the same roof. She heard doors slamming, kids running, and animal noises all day and night. Her daddy, Bobby Jones kept promising her that he was going to get them out of their apartment very soon. As long as Reece could remember, this had always been their home. So for Reece, her dad's "soon" couldn't come soon enough.

Although Reece was her mother's only child, she had overhead that she had two siblings on her dad's side. One of her dad's other kids was much older than her. He was hardly ever discussed. The other was a younger brother who was turning five. Reece quickly learned as a young kid what philandering meant. She had overheard her mother, Joyce tell Aunt Patsy that she was going to save up some money and finally leave St. Louis without her dad. Perhaps that was why her mother decided to do hair on the side every time daddy was out of town on one of his trucking routes.

Reece's dad would leave for weeks at a time, and a few times he didn't come home for a few months. He claimed he had big jobs in different countries. Although her mom never talked to Reece about it, it was obvious to Reece that those missing months were around the time her little brother was conceived. Reece was around five at the time, but she still remembered how Aunt Patsy talked about her dad being a manipulator and a philandering whore.

As she got older, Reece came to know what those words meant from the many times her dad was caught cheating. However, it had seemed to become a normalcy for them. Dad would mess up and mom would threaten to leave. He would come home bearing apologies, gifts, and money, then mom would take him back. Who could blame him? As gorgeous as mom was, who would let her go?

Despite lingering issues with her mom, her dad treated her like a princess. Nothing was off limits for Reece. He took her places, played games with her, and had genuine father-daughter conversations with her. Then like clockwork, he was back out on the road again leaving Reece to deal with the disgruntled mother that he created. It became emotionally draining for her mom as well as Reece. Reece wished that one of them would do something different because she was tired of having to stay outside so much lately.

Although Reece was generally an obedient child, she couldn't hide her disdain from having to stay outside all day. Joyce had explained to her that she didn't want any of her new male clients staring at her ten-year-old daughter. The explanation didn't make any sense to Reese. Why would a grownup stare at her? Furthermore, she could go to the back room as opposed to sitting outside for long periods of time, sometimes even hours.

At times, it was fun hanging out on the playground. Swinging was her favorite thing until twenty other kids came out there with her. It was the 90's, so kids being outside was practically the only past time kids had. Most of the time Reece sat in peace and read mystery books on the steps. She would even sneak and read some of her mother's old romance novels. Reading had become her new escape. At least it was until one of her nosey neighbors would come out and interrupted her.

"How come y'all be having all them folks come in and out y'all house?" One of Reece's nine-year-old acquaintances walked up and asked.

"Duhh, Brittani. You already know that my momma do hair."

"Well, Keisha told me that Jason told her that his momma's cousin told him that yo momma not doing that much hair."

"First of all, Jason or whoever don't know shit about what goes on in my momma's house. Jason just mad because his momma got nappy hair anyways."

"You don't have to get an attitude with me, Reece, I was just saying."

"Well, I'm just saying y'all need to mind y'all own damn business."

"I'ma tell yo momma you out here cussin'."
Brittani warned, leaving behind a sassy walk while slamming the main complex door.

"You little idiot," Reece whispered underneath her breath.

Besides the fact of knowing that her mom wouldn't do anything even if she did know what Reece was outside saying, Brittani knew that she made an empty threat. Joyce didn't allow any kids knocking on her door. Her mother didn't even like the neighborhood kids. She had a spray bottle ready if she saw any kids through her peephole. Half of the time Reece wondered how her mother truly felt about her. She wasn't mean or abusive, but she lacked the nurturing aspect expected of a mother. In fact, she acted more like an older sister. She never hugged Reese, kissed her, or took her places like her dad did. Reece couldn't even remember the last time her mother told her that she loved her.

When Reece turned seven, her mother even told her to call her by her first name. She said momma made her sound too old. At first, it was weird saying "bye Joyce" when she left for school, but Reece got used to it. However, she secretly wanted to just call her momma like the other kids called their moms.

About thirty minutes later, the same guy that was at Reece's door earlier walked past her. His hair was now neatly shaved on the sides and in the back, opposed to the full Afro he had when he first entered the apartment. Contrary to her mother's belief, he didn't pay any attention to her. He walked by without saying a word or even looking in her direction. It was almost like he didn't know she existed.

She walked into the apartment and saw Joyce sweeping up hair from the kitchen floor. The room was saturated with air freshener and the television was unusually loud. Joyce seemed startled when Reece shut the door.

"Didn't I tell you to wait until I called you in here?"

"I was tired of sitting on that hard concrete, so I came in once I saw your client leave."

"Well, next time wait anyway. A few minutes wasn't gonna kill you."

"How come I just can't go in my room and close the door? I get tired of dealing with these kids in this building."

"When you start helping me pay bills you can help make decisions."

"But when that man came out the apartment door, he didn't look at me. I don't think he knew I existed."

"Reece, if I say stay outside then that's what I mean and I don't wanna hear nothing else about it."

"But Joyce, it's hot out there and-"

"Shut up and go to your room!" She yelled.

Without another word, Reece looked down at the floor and slowly exited the kitchen. It was normal for Joyce to yell at her when she was already in a bad mood. Reece figured that client had done something to make her mad. So when Reece saw the brown wallet slightly visible from under the couch, she didn't say anything. She figured it belonged to the man that just left, so she discreetly nudged it farther under the couch with her foot before heading to her room. Thanks to him, not only did she get yelled at, but she had to stay in her room until it was time to eat. She hoped that the man would get pulled over and arrested for not having his license with him.

Chapter 2

The next day, Reece woke up to the smell of bacon, toast, and perhaps sausage from her bed. Her mother didn't normally cook a big breakfast during the summer, so there had to be something taking place. Either her mom felt bad about yelling at her or they were having guests.

Reece promptly rose from her bed and went to go brush her teeth. She had a feeling today was going to be a great day. She wondered what her mom would do if she unexpectedly gave her a hug. Perhaps Joyce didn't know she wanted to be hugged. Maybe her mom thought that she had grown out of it. Today she was going to show her that she hadn't.

Reece slowly moved up the hall in the direction of the kitchen. She couldn't believe that she was getting nervous about giving her mom a hug. Surely she wouldn't reject it, would she? As she got closer to the front room, she heard a familiar voice.

"Daddy!" She yelled, jumping into his arms.

"Hey baby girl. It's about time you woke up from your beauty sleep."

"Daddy, when did you get here? Why didn't you wake me sooner?"

"I wanted it to be a surprise."

"Well, you did it, daddy," she smiled, hugging him again.

"You act like you haven't seen the man in years," Joyce stated.

"Aww, don't be like that. She misses her daddy, just like I miss my little princess." He responded, giving her a kiss on the head.

"Daddy, I didn't know you were coming in this week. What did you bring me?"

"Is daddy's gifts the only things you missed?"

"No, daddy, but you always bring me something sooo...that's what I expect."

"That's what you expect, huh? Girl, you are a replica of your momma," he laughed, pulling out a box.

"Wow! It's a Nintendo GameBoy, Joyce!"

"Reece, what has gotten into you? You're not grown. You don't call your momma by her first name," Bobby stated.

"But-"

"Reece, go wash your hands so you can eat breakfast," Joyce quickly interrupted.

Reece did as instructed and slowly walked back down the hall. She was pissed beyond belief. *Why didn't Joyce just tell him that's what she told her to do?* The nerve of her to let daddy get on to her for no reason. It wasn't her fault that daddy liked hugs and she didn't. Once she had daddy alone, Reece had planned to tell him that she was ordered to call her by her first name.

The talking was minimal at the breakfast table and Reece wasn't sure why. Aside from the times he was caught cheating, her mother would normally be happy when dad was home. Dad acted like he hadn't eaten in weeks while her mom side-eyed him in annoyance. Dad caught her glares a few times, but didn't say anything. Perhaps something happened that made him come home early. They obviously weren't going to tell her, so Reece figured she'd find out later whenever her mom talked to Aunt Patsy.

"How about I take the most beautiful girl in the world to The Game World arcade today?"

"Oh my gosh, dad! Do you really mean it?"

"Yeah, if it's okay with your mother."

"Uh...mom. Can I go?"

"Sure," Joyce dryly responded, still looking down at her plate.

"Perhaps you can com with us, Joyce. We could make this a family venture," Bobby suggested.

"I have more things to do than fool around at kiddy land," she replied.

"Like what?"

"Like be a parent."

"Being a parent involves doing fun things with your child and not having your child refer to you on a first name basis," Bobby argued.

"I think being a parent is providing stability for your child and not having illegitimate children scattered across the country."

"You have some nerve to sit up here and act like I don't pay every got damn bill in this place while you sit on yo ass and gossip to your nosey ass sister everyday."

"Well, why don't you leave and take your daughter with you. I can handle all these bills by my damn self."

Just as Bobby was about to respond, the phone rang. Joyce picked it up, but promptly hung up after hello. It rang again, but she promptly hung up.

"Who was that?" He asked.

"A bill collector."

"A bill collector? What bill was it for?"

"I obviously hung up before I got that information."

"Well, what company did they say?" Bobby continued to question.

"I don't know, Sherlock. It was a recording."

"Didn't I send you money a few weeks ago to get everything paid up?"

"That's your problem. You have a bad habit of sending me what you think I should have and not what I need."

"Well, what else do you need, Joyce?"

They all sat in silence for a minute as Reece watched her dad begin to tap his fingers on the table. He stared at Joyce as if he was trying to read her mind. Reece couldn't remember her dad ever being upset, but this time it seemed as if he was. His look was very stern and unforgiving. He looked like he was trying to keep himself from exploding. Reece didn't understand why he was so upset. They got calls from bill collectors all of the time. Luckily, dad was usually on the road. If he was getting upset over one call, Reece could only imagine how he would react if he was home all week.

"Reece, go wash up and put on those clothes I picked out for you so daddy can take you out, okay?"

Reece promptly nodded and walked towards the back. She heard her dad slam the front door as he exited the apartment. While she was getting her clothes from her dresser, she saw her dad in front of the apartment complex from her window pacing back and forth with a cigarette in his mouth. At this point, Reece assumed that this was bigger than a call from a bill collector. She wondered had her dad seen hair on the floor from the client that was there earlier. Her mom told her to never tell dad about her hair clients, but he must have suspected something. He knew that Joyce didn't have a job, so he probably wondered how was she going to be able to pay the bills on her own?

After showering and getting dressed, Reece headed to the front room where her mom was sitting. After a brief look, she noticed that her dad still wasn't in the apartment. With a disappointing look on her face, she sat down in the armchair.

"Straighten your face up before I make you stay at home. Your dad is still outside waiting on you."

Like a bouncy spring, she jumped up, quickly hugged her mom, and kissed her on the cheek. She headed towards the door before her mom could change her mind.

"Reece."

"Ma'am?" She responded, halfway out of the door.

"I love you."

Reece paused. Her mom's words were totally unexpected. Perhaps she should have hugged and kissed her mother a long time ago. Perhaps dad made things right again. Whatever it was, Reece was glad it happened.

"I love you, too...mom."

Chapter 3

Reece walked downstairs and spotted her dad sitting in the driver's side of his truck with the door opened. She happily hopped into the passenger seat and waited while her dad put his cigarette out on the ground. He sprayed a mist of peach cream fragrance to cover the lingering smoke.

"You ready to go, Muffin?" He asked, closing his door and adjusting his rearview mirror.

"Dad, I thought you were going to give me a new name. Muffin sounds so childish now that I'm older and more responsible."

"Why are you in such a big hurry to grow up so fast?"

"I'm not. It's just..."

Reece figured that this would be the perfect time to tell dad that her mom told her to call her on a first name basis. It was obvious he didn't understand the nature of their relationship since he was gone most of the time. She then thought it may be better not to tell him. She didn't want him to go back and tell Joyce what she had said and make the person that she had to go home to mad at her again.

"It's just what, Babydoll?"

"Well, I think my maturity level has increased like mom said. Therefore, some of the old kiddy things that I used to like should be done away with."

"Wow...well, I guess since you put it that way then I can dig it."

"Good. I'm glad we have an understanding, daddy."

"Did you really just say that you're glad we have an understanding?" He laughed. "You really are your mother's child."

"Dad, you always say that."

"I do, don't I? Babydoll, let me ask you something. Perhaps you can help your ole dad get an understanding of a few things."

"Okay, dad. Shoot."

"Well, your mother and I had a talk before you woke up this morning. She said she was unhappy and wanted to get away. Has mommy been talking to you about going somewhere?"

"No. Joyce...I mean...mom, doesn't talk to me about much of anything. She tells Aunt Patsy how she feels."

"Has she said anything to Aunt Patsy lately?"

"Uhh...well, Aunt Patsy wants us to move back home with her. Mom said no because she didn't have enough money saved yet."

"Oh. When did your mom start saving money?"

"When she started cutting hair."

Before Reece realized it, the words had already slipped from her mouth. Joyce was going to be furious once she found out that she told her dad. She had to figure out a way to make things sound reasonable.

"She only did it a few times though. The electric bill had gotten too high and we were low on food. Don't be mad at her, daddy. You were out of the country, so she had no choice."

Bobby quickly glanced at Reece then focused his attention back on the road. The frown lines in his head were beginning to form, so Reece knew he was upset or in deep thought.

"You're not going to fuss at her, are you dad? Cause if you do, she's definitely going to come down hard on me."

"No, my little Princess. I'm not going to fuss at the person who takes care of my little heart."

"Well, could you do one last favor for your little heart and don't tell mom that I told you. She can go days without talking to me when she's mad."

Once again her dad glanced over at her with a confused look on his face. *Had he really not known this entire time that some of his actions played a role in how her mother dealt with her?* For the first time ever, Reece saw a tear form in her dad's eye.

"Well, you know what baby girl?" He began, brushing off his momentary sadness, "Daddy is going to take you out and show you the best time ever. Daddy is gonna make everything better, okay?"

"Okay, daddy."

Hours later, Reece was still giddy about the wonderful day she had. Not only did daddy take her to the arcade, he took her to get pizza and ice-cream. To top it all off, he bought her a gold necklace and a pendant that said 'Love' with her birthstone inside the 'o' letter. She couldn't remember the last time she had spent the entire day with her dad. It felt like it was her birthday.

Later that night before tucking Reece into bed, Bobby explained that he had to leave in the wee hours of the night. He said that he'd be gone by the time she got out of bed in the morning, so he gave her another tight hug and said he'd call once he got to his destination. After a goodnight kiss on the forehead, he told her he loved her and closed the door. It didn't take long for Reece to roll over in a blissful dream.

A few hours later, Reece woke up in a cold sweat. She seemed to have a nightmare and couldn't go back to sleep. She noticed her bedroom door was slightly opened and a seemingly cooler breeze began to spread throughout her room. She looked at her tiny clock on the side of her bed that read 3:47 a.m.

She rested her head back on her pillow in hopes of falling back to sleep. The more she tried, the stranger she felt. She was certain that daddy had closed her door before he left, so how was it open? Perhaps her mom had checked in on her last night to make sure she was asleep so she and dad could do grownup things.

Reece was suddenly startled by a loud thump from inside the apartment. She instantly jumped out of bed and kneeled down beside it. She remembered how her mom had talked about there being some robberies throughout the complex a few months back. Reece wasn't sure what to do, so she quickly hid under her bed.

Several minutes of complete silence had passed as Reece lay still under the bed. She hadn't heard any additional noises, but she wasn't sure if it was safe yet. She then wondered what room had the noise come from and if her mom had heard it? Then another terrifying thought crossed her mind. What if her mom had fallen and needed help?

Reece eased from under the bed and quietly pushed open her door. She noticed her mom's door was closed, so she probably slept through it. Maybe the noise wasn't as loud as she presumed it to be. Perhaps the noise came from outside or another apartment. The neighbors were always making noises all through the day and night. *Silly me*, she thought.

Before going back to bed, Reece figured she'd get a drink of water for her dry mouth. Still trying not to wake her mom, Reece tiptoed up the hallway. Joyce always left the oven lamp on in the kitchen just in case. Reece's heart almost flew from her chest once again when she saw her mom on the couch. The television was on, but her mother's head was turned away from the screen.

Quickly getting over her fright, something was weird about the way her mom was positioned. One leg was hanging off of the couch while her right arm was stretched out in mid air. As Reece fully rounded the corner, she also noticed the front door was wide open. A sudden chill ran up Reece's spine. She ran to the door and quickly closed it.

"Mom?" She whispered, edging over towards the couch, but stopping at a short distance. Her heart was beating so fast that it felt as if it was about to fall out of her chest. "Mom, are you woke?"

With no response, Reece edged a tad bit closer to her mom and noticed that her eyes were closed. She definitely appeared to be in a deep sleep. The last thing she wanted to do was wake her mom from a pleasant dream. She would be pissed for days. Not knowing what to do, she sat at the kitchen table to see if her mom would eventually wake up on her own.

It wasn't long before Reece decided to slowly walk back over towards the couch. She sat down on the love seat that was adjacent to the sofa. She purposely knocked the remote from the table to the floor to see if she would get a reaction. There was still no movement. She picked up the remote and turned up the volume as loud as it would go. She quickly turned it down after nothing happened.

As frightening as the situation was, Reece could no longer suppress her inner thoughts. She sat directly in front of her mom and focused on her chest. She didn't see it move. Shaking with fear, she began to tear up as she reached out her trembling hand to touch her mother's face. Her skin was cold. Reece screamed in agony as she grabbed the phone and dialed 911.

Chapter 4

Reece rocked back and forth while waiting on the phone with the operator for the police to arrive. It wasn't until the operator had asked was there anyone else with her that Reece had realized she had no one else. She never considered anything happening to her mom, so living with someone else hadn't occurred to her.

Once the police had arrived, they also began to ask Reece a series of questions. She told them that she heard a loud noise when she woke up, but she didn't hear or see anything else. The police weren't sure what loud noise she could have heard since her mom had likely been strangled judging from the marks around her neck. They had also observed that her mom had been deceased for a few hours according to her body temperature.

She overheard the police try to contact dad's truck phone, but they were unsuccessful. The only other relatives that Reece was acquainted with were Aunt Patsy and dad's brother, Uncle Mason. Uncle Mason was definitely the black sheep of the family, but he was always dependable.

Uncle Mason had two live-in girlfriends and he ran a strip club in Kansas City, Missouri. Joyce wasn't fond of him because she thought that he badly influenced dad, so Reece didn't get to go to his house often. However, Uncle Mason treated Reece almost as good as dad did. The times that they did go visit, Uncle Mason would literally have stacks of presents for her. Joyce hated when her daddy bragged about Uncle Mason's new house. Reece couldn't wait to see it.

Reece watched as the coroners placed her mom on a stretcher. She overheard one of them say how much of a shame it was to lose such a beautiful life as they slowly began to carry her out of the apartment. One of the coroners noticed that Reece was looking, so he told the other guy not to cover her mom's face. Even in death, Reece also thought her mom looked ravishing. She looked like Dorothy Dandridge lying fast asleep. From that moment, that's how Reece decided to remember her mom. She decided not to think of her as dead, but peacefully sleeping.

"We know that this is scary for you, but we need you to remember everything that you possibly can before you went to sleep last night," the detective said in a calm voice as he kneeled in front of Reece.

"I remember that my daddy tucked me in and said he would be leaving early. After that, I went to sleep."

"Do you remember what time that was?"

"Uh...I would say it was around ten o'clock when I finally fell asleep."

"Where was your mom when your daddy tucked you into bed?"

"Uhm... I think she was here in the living room."

"Did she say anything to you or daddy before you went to sleep?"

"Not really. She was watching one of her favorite shows when we got home. Daddy brought me home kinda late, so she told me to wash up and go to bed."

"Did your mom seem upset?"

"No."

"How about your dad? Did he seem upset or mad at mommy?"

"No. Daddy hardly ever gets mad. He had to get back on the road for his trucking gig."

"Is there anything at all you can remember about yesterday that seemed different?"

Reece paused. She had mentally begun to recall her day yesterday. Nothing seemed out of the ordinary. Her dad had popped up early, but that was something that he normally did. He never showed up at the time that he said he would. Her mom had her clients, but that wasn't unusual either. Then she thought about it. That man that she thought who had made her mom upset had left his wallet. Reece remembered that she had kicked it under the couch.

The detective asked where was she going as Reece slowly rose from the loveseat. She bent down and looked under the sofa in the direction where she had kicked the wallet. After scouring underneath the entire couch, there was nothing there. *Where was the wallet?*

"Are you looking for something in particular?" The detective asked.

"Yeah. There was a wallet here yesterday that a man had left."

"Do you mean your dad?"

"Well, no. My dad isn't just a man. He's my dad."

"Could you describe this man?"

"I only really seen him from the back and a little from the side. He had an Afro until my mom cut his hair. He was tall, brown-skinned, and he had on a white t-shirt with gray jogging pants."

"Did you see what kind of car he drove?"

"It was a big blue, two-door car with weird triangular shaped windows in the back."

"Perfect. We really appreciate your help and we're going to find the bad person that did this, okay?"

"Okay."

"We've also contacted your aunt and we're going to have her pick you up from the police station. In the meantime, I want you to go get some things from your room that you may need."

"What's going to happen to my mom's things?"

"Uh...well, the other detectives have to do a little more investigating on the apartment. After they're done, they'll call your aunt or your dad to get the rest of the things. Hopefully, we will have gotten in contact with your dad by then."

"Oh...okay. Officer?"

"Yes?"

"When you find the bad guy, make sure that you tell him that I said may God have mercy on his soul."

Chapter 5

The officers down at the precinct took a quick liking to Reece as they fed her donuts and tried to keep her entertained with crossword puzzles. One officer even took it upon himself to show her a few magic tricks. Even though she had seen and knew the basis of all the tricks, she pretended to be entertained so they wouldn't stop being nice.

It wasn't long before Aunt Patsy had arrived at the police station in her pajamas with her hair tied up in a scarf. Reece was slightly confused because she was under the impression that Aunt Patsy stayed about three and a half hours away in Indianapolis. She saw Aunt Patsy being escorted to another area by the police. Perhaps they needed to identify who she was.

After about 30 minutes, Aunt Patsy came around the corner with the same detective that had spoken with Reece. It appeared as if she had been crying, but Reece wasn't really sure. She hadn't seen her aunt since she was around five or six, so they didn't have a close bond. If it wasn't for her mother constantly talking to Patsy on the phone, she wouldn't know much about her at all.

Aunt Patsy didn't smile or try to console Reece at the least. She told her to grab her things and to follow her. After snatching the bag out of Reece's hand and throwing it in the trunk of her car, she ordered Reece to get in the back seat and not say a word.

Throughout the drive, Reece noticed her aunt cutting her eyes at her through the rear view mirror. It was almost as if Aunt Patsy was trying to make her feel uncomfortable. Instead of asking questions, Reece remained quiet in the back seat. Perhaps this was just a weird way that her aunt grieved.

"I hope you're happy now. You're the reason why your mom is gone," Patsy stated.

"What?"

"Don't you 'what' me little girl. You say yes ma'am!" she screamed. "Say it!"

"But it wasn't my fault," Reece whined, totally confused.

"You just wait a minute."

About five minutes later, Patsy pulled over at a gas station. She got out of the car, came around to Reece's side, and slapped her in the face after opening the door. Reece instantly began to cry. Luckily, a bystander saw the incident and called the police to report child abuse. Although the bystander gave a description of the car, she wasn't able to get Aunt Patsy's license plate number.

Two hours later after sitting in the car with her face covered, Reece was snatched out and pushed to the ground by Aunt Patsy. She then grabbed Reece's bag and threw it on top of her. Aunt Patsy must have heard her kids opening the door, so she ordered Reece to get up off the ground.

"Hey, Reece. Do you remember me?" Asked Reece's eleven-year-old cousin, Tasha.

Reece tried to force a smile, but she couldn't. She didn't understand why Aunt Patsy was being so cruel towards her. Tears began to well in her eyes. She did not want to go into that house.

"Aunt Joyce just died, so she's sad," Patsy said. "Get her bags and help her get situated in the house."

Tasha put her arms around Reece and escorted her inside. She sat down on the couch next to a little girl she hadn't ever met.

"This is your little cousin, Asia. She's three, so you haven't met her yet," Tasha said. "Say hello, Asia."

"Hello, Asia," the toddler repeated and snickered.

"I'm sorry to hear about Aunt Joyce. She was always so sweet to me. Asia really didn't get to know her. Aunt Joyce only really had seen Asia one time at the hospital when she was born."

"Oh." Reece softly responded.

"I hope you don't stay sad for long. Anything that's mine is yours," Tasha continued, giving Reece a one armed hug.

Reece forced a half smile and briefly leaned her head on Tasha. She began to relax a little more from her cousin's friendly demeanor. As they talked a little more, Reece looked around the nicely decorated living room and pictures on the wall. Tasha retrieved a photo album from the table to show Reece more pictures.

Reece saw a picture of her mom, grandma, and Aunt Patsy all smiling together. It was obvious that they were younger, but mom still looked the same. She suddenly cracked a full smile. Her focus then went towards a picture of a young man.

"Is this my dad?" Reece asked.

"Your dad? No silly. This is our older brother, Byron. He doesn't live with us though. He's much older than us."

"No you are not sittin' on my couch with those dirty ass pants." Aunt Patsy yelled, interrupting their moment. "Come here." She demanded, pulling Reece to the floor.

Patsy pulled out a belt and began spanking Reece in front of her cousins. Reece hollered in agony from the hard licks that were hitting her arms and legs. Although her mom yelled at her from time to time, she never got a whooping or any type of physical punishment. The kids were horrified. Baby Asia screamed as she ran behind the couch.

"Mom, stop! What are you doing? You are hurting her!" Tasha yelled.

"Don't you ever question me," threaten Patsy, popping Tasha on the hand with the belt.

"Ouch." Tasha yelled, reacting from the slight sting.

Patsy threw the belt on the floor and walked out of the room. Although the baby was clearly without understanding, Tasha quickly realized that her mom had it out for Reece, but she wasn't sure why. She sat down next to Reece and put her arms around her in attempt to console her.

"Where is your dad?" Tasha whispered.

Reece shrugged her shoulders as she continued to wipe her tears. Baby Asia also came over and gave Reece a hug.

All through the day, Reece wasn't allowed to do anything, but sit on the floor. She had to ask permission to go to the bathroom and she had to face away from the television. Despite her mom's evilness towards Reece, Tasha had no problem keeping her company. She decided not to watch television either. However, every time baby Asia would give Reece a toy so that she could play with her, Patsy would snatch it from baby Asia and hit Reece with the belt. This quickly discouraged the baby from coming near Reece.

The next day, Reece was ordered to go sit in the closet while they all ate breakfast. An hour later, Patsy brought her a half eaten biscuit and water in a Sippy cup. That was the only thing that Reece had eaten since the donuts at the police station yesterday, so she devoured it.

The next few days went the exact same way. Patsy had embedded in Reece's head that her dad had abandoned her and would never come back to see her. Patsy even made Reece sleep in the girl's bedroom closet. Although Patsy's kids weren't on the receiving end of the abuse, their spirits were down as well.

One night while eating dinner, Reece asked could she be excused from the floor to her closet. Normally, she had to wait until the kids finished their food and eat whatever they didn't eat. Unknown to Patsy, Tasha would sneak Reece extra food once everyone was in bed.

"Reece, I brought you some Oreo cookies and a peanut butter sandwich."

"I'm not hungry tonight, Tasha. But thank you anyways."

"Well, I'll wrap it up and hide it in the refrigerator. I'll say it's mine if she finds it."

"Thanks," Reece responded as she turned and faced the wall.

"Here is your pillow and a blanket. As usual, I'll come get them before momma wakes up," Tasha whispered and left, sensing Reece's sadness.

Reece wished that this was all a horrific nightmare, but she obviously knew it wasn't. Aunt Patsy clearly wasn't a sane human being. She was pure evil. Reece had just lost her mom, her dad was never coming back, and now she had to be abused for the rest of her life.

Reece had decided at that point that she was going to run away from there. She thought about how the police may find her and send her back to her aunt who would beat her even worse. She would rather live in a pig hole than with her aunt. Better yet, Reece decided that she wanted to die. Tomorrow, when Aunt Patsy wasn't paying attention, she was going to run out of the house into the middle of the busy intersection and attempt to get run over by a car.

Chapter 6

The next day, Reece was awakened by a violent snatching. Aunt Patsy had grabbed her from the closet and threw her against the wall. Reece was petrified. *Why hadn't Tasha got the covers and pillows like she was supposed to? Did she want her to get beat?* But something was different. Aunt Patsy was huffing as if she had been running. She had the same fear in her eyes as Reece had when she first got here.

"You listen here you little shit. You'd better not say anything about what goes on around here or I'll kill you dead. Do you understand? You have to come back here when your dad goes to jail."

"Babydoll." A voice called from the front room.

Hearing her dad's voice was like a thousands Angels playing violins in a beautiful harmony. She felt the weight lifting from her body. Perhaps it was her pushing Patsy's arms out of the way in order to run to her dad.

"Daddy! Daddy! Daddy!" She cried, running into his arms and holding him tight.

"Babydoll, you're shaking. What's wrong?"

"She just got into an argument with one of the girls. You know how girls are." Patsy stated.

Bobby instantly looked at the girls who were sitting on the sofa. Baby Asia tilted her head back in shyness while Tasha stared blankly at Reece. Bobby was a long way from being a dummy. He could tell something was sketchy.

"No...no...I don't know. These girls were in here and Reece was in the back. Besides, Reece isn't going to get into with a baby."

"I'm talking about Tasha. Look, don't come up in my house questioning me about my kids."

"Oh, I see you got it confused. This one here isn't yours," Bobby said, moving Reece to the side.

"She's mine until further notice. The paperwork says you can take her to Joyce's funeral, but you need to have her back here by nightfall tomorrow."

"I wanna go to Aunt Joyce's funeral," Tasha softly stated.

"You shut up. Y'all ain't going nowhere. Have her back on time or I'll call the law." Patsy threatened.

Bobby kneeled down and gave his attention back to his daughter. "Listen Babydoll, I have a few errands to run, but I promise to come back and get you in the morning. I brought your dress, so you can be ready, okay?"

Reece looked at Aunt Patsy who gave her an intimidating look. She also looked at Tasha who cut her eyes at Bobby and then back to her. Tasha grabbed baby Asia's hand, walked over to Reece, and they both hugged her. Without another word, Tasha walked down the hall towards their room as baby Asia looked back until she was out of view. Reece wasn't sure if this was some type of signal from Tasha, but she definitely took it as one.

"Daddy, I have to tell you something."

"You shut your little mouth and don't you go telling lies," Patsy interrupted, walking towards Reece while pointing her finger in Reece's face.

"Have you lost your got damn mind?" Bobby yelled, pushing Patsy back.

"That's it! I'm calling the police."

Bobby quickly snatched the phone from Patsy's grasp. She put her hands up in defense mode as if Bobby was going to hit her. Something happened and it was obvious to him that Patsy was trying to hide it. He threw the phone against the wall and shattered it into pieces.

"What did you have to tell daddy, Babydoll?"

"Daddy, Aunt Patsy hates me! She slapped me in the car. She pushed me to the ground and whooped me for sitting on her couch. She feeds me their scraps and makes me sleep on the floor in the girl's closet. She calls me stupid and slaps me if I try to watch television. The baby is even afraid to play with me because she knows I'll get punished. I hate it here, daddy. Please daddy, don't make me stay," she cried. "I'd rather die."

Bobby didn't know what to do. He tried to process everything his daughter said. He fell to his knees and silently cried with his face in his hand. He couldn't believe that his child had endured so much agony by her own flesh and blood.

With one swipe to his face, Bobby lifted his head. "Babydoll, I am so sorry that I wasn't here to protect you. I had no idea that this would happen. You don't have to ever see this wicked woman again or even call her your aunt. She's nothing from this point forward, okay?"

"Now that y'all done had y'all little Kumbaya moment-"

Before Pasty could finish her sentence, Bobby snapped. "You been fuckin' locking my daughter in a got damn closet and putting ya filthy hands on her! I should snap ya fuckin' neck right now," Bobby yelled, grabbing Aunt Patsy around the neck and pushing her against the wall.

"Get yo nasty ass hands off of me before I have yo ass locked up!" She barely choked out, attempting to free herself.

Reece could see her aunt's face turning a reddish/blue color as her dad tightened his grip. Although her aunt tortured her, she wasn't sure if she could watch her die. Despite her cruel ways, Aunt Patsy was still a part of her mom. Besides, she didn't want baby Asia and Tasha to lose their mom, too. It was all too much.

"Daddy," Reece said, walking over to him and gently touching his arm. "I can't lose you, too. Who's gonna protect me?"

Bobby looked down at his daughter and then back up at Patsy. Through his peripheral vision, he also noticed Reece's cousins standing at the end of the hall. He slowly loosened his grip as he pushed her back towards the wall and released her. She instantly fell while coughing and still gasping.

"If you ever come near my daughter again, I will kill you. Dead ass! Reece...go get your bags."

"Fuck you, Bobby. Ain't nobody scared of yo bitch ass. Get out of my house and take that heifer with you." She coughed out, drooling saliva and blood. "You wasn't shit to Joyce just like you ain't shit to Byron."

Bobby grabbed Reece's hand and walked out of the door. The secret was out and the truth was ugly. Although it made no sense to Reece at first, it became clear why she was Aunt Patsy's most hated target. Byron was not only her older cousin, but he was also her daddy's son.

Chapter 7

After the funeral, Bobby, Reece, Uncle Mason and his girlfriends all went out to eat at a steakhouse. Aunt Patsy didn't show as expected. Joyce's parents had died before Reece was born. Aside from a few neighbors and cousins that Reece hadn't met, they were the only ones who attended the memorial service.

Reece felt weird about her thoughts towards her mom. She was definitely going to miss her, but she couldn't understand why her tears were minimal. Perhaps the reality hadn't sunk in yet. Besides, Uncle Mason was so outgoing and funny, that it was hard for Reece to even think about being sad.

"Reece, how do you feel about staying with Uncle Mason, Juliet, and Jade?" Her dad asked.

It was a very unexpected question. Although Reece was aware that they weren't going to stay at a hotel for the rest of her life, the idea of staying with Uncle Mason was new. Apparently, Uncle Mason and his girlfriends weren't aware either. The ladies quickly looked at each other while Uncle Mason nearly choked on his steak.

"Uh... I didn't know that was the plan," Reece finally responded.

"Bo, let me holla at'cha on the sideline real quick." Uncle Mason said in a demanding tone.

Uncle Mason smiled at Reece as he and her dad excused themselves from the table. Once outside, Reece could see Uncle Mason put his hands on his hips while her dad held his hands out in an explanatory manner. She really liked Uncle Mason, so she was more than happy to live with him. Anything was better than staying with Aunt Patsy.

"Well...Reece, I guess you're going to be staying with us for a while." One of Uncle Mason's girlfriends said. "You can call me Aunt Juliet if you like."

"Uh...if it's okay, can I call you Miss Juliet? The aunt thing brings back too many bad memories."

"Oh, okay. Juliet is fine, Sweetie. It's whatever you're comfortable with."

Ms Juliet seems so nice and friendly, thought Reece. She was almost just as beautiful as mom. She had golden skin with long, shiny black hair and a smile to die for. Jade on the other hand was more reserved. She didn't talk much and she kept her head down a lot. She was cute, but not nearly as pretty as Juliet. Reece wondered why Uncle Mason needed two girlfriends when Juliet was so pretty and nice.

"Alright, Cupcake. You're gonna stay with Uncle Mason for a while until I can find a local gig. I spoke with my boss already and things are looking good. He said that there should be plenty of work in Kansas City."

"So…Kansas City will be our permanent home, huh? Well, that's cool. We'll be closer to Uncle Mason."

"Uh...uh...yeah. I guess that's it."

The moment was awkward and Uncle Mason had stopped talking altogether. He didn't have any kids, so maybe he was worried about being able to take care of her. She definitely didn't want Uncle Mason to see her as a hassle.

"Don't worry, Uncle Mason, I got you. I can cook my own food, I know how to do my own hair, I do laundry and know how to keep myself entertained. I'm a very self-sufficient person, so you won't even know I'm there."

Stunned by her statement, all the adults looked at her as if they were impressed. Even Jade curled up her lips for a brief moment. Bobby knew his daughter was smart, but her intelligence superseded that of a ten-year-old.

"Someone buy this young lady a martini," Uncle Mason joked.

Just like that, the mood had change. Everyone was talking again, even Jade. After they were done eating, Reece was able to go back to her former home. She collected a few of her mom's things that she deemed as important and said a silent prayer. As she stood in her mom's room, it had finally set in that she was never going to see her again. Tears began to flow down her cheeks.

"Come on, Babydoll," her dad softly whispered, putting his arms around her.

Just like that, it was over. There was no more Aunt Patsy, no more mom, or sitting on the front stoop of her apartment for hours. Reece was entering into an unknown world with Uncle Mason and his two polar opposite girlfriends.

"Wake up, Cupcakes."

Reece opened her eyes to sound of Uncle Mason's chipper tone. She hadn't realized she slept the entire four hour drive to Kansas City. When she looked around, she saw rolling hills and a huge white mansion.

"Where are we, Uncle Mason?"

"We're at home, Cupcake. Mi casa, su casa."

"You live here?" Reece asked, not believing what she saw. "This is like something out of a magazine! You must own about fifty strip clubs?"

"Listen to you making your old uncle blush." He paused and briefly cut his eyes at Juliet. "Uh...how did you know I have a strip club," he asked, clearing his throat.

"My mom told me. I also heard her tell Aunt Patsy that daddy used to help you flip the women until she got pregnant. What does that mean?"

"Uh...why don't we get out so you can have a look around." Juliet interrupted.

"You bet…Juliet."

Reece hopped out of her uncle's black Chevy Suburban and looked around at the endless green grass. In the center of the yard was a huge statue of an angel with water lightly flowing from both hands. Reece walked over to the statue and touched the angel's feet. It was a moment that almost brought Uncle Mason and his girlfriends to tears.

"Uh...Cupcake. How about we go see the inside of the house?"

"Sure Uncle Mason. I'll grab my things."

"Of course you won't. Our helper, Paulette will get those for you."

"Whoa...you have a maid, Uncle Mason?"

"I wouldn't call them maids. They're more like family that help around the house when Uncle Mason gets very busy."

Reece was under the impression that the girlfriends did the chores since Uncle Mason had two of them. Not wanting to offend anyone, she kept her thoughts to herself. After being escorted around the extravagant home, Uncle Mason took Reece to her room on the second floor.

Her golden canopy bed was laced with white and gold curtains with the same color pillows and comforter to match. She had two huge dressers, two chests, and an enormous walk-in closet that was about the size of her old room at her apartment. On the walls were two large pictures of ballerinas dancing opposite of one another in golden frames. Needless to say, it was a room fit for a princess.

"Wow! I feel like I'm dreaming, Uncle Mason."

Reece turned around and saw Jade standing in the door instead of her uncle.

"Where's Uncle Mason?" Reece asked, puzzled as to why Jade was staring at her.

"He had to go and take care of some business, but he'll be back when he gets back. Feel free to look around, but don't mess anything up. This is my daughter's room."

"Oh, can I meet her?"

Jade walked off without responding. Reece had been getting bad vibes from her since they met. However, Reece was confident that Uncle Mason wouldn't allow anything bad to happen to her.

It didn't take long for Reece to get into the routine of things. She'd wake up every morning to a prepared breakfast, go to a kickboxing class, have lunch with Uncle Mason and/or Juliet, help do a few chores around the house, and take swimming lessons with her private instructor outback in the lap pool. In the evening before dinner, she also had a private tutor to learn Spanish. When school started, the routine didn't change much. Uncle Mason told her that keeping her active would keep her out of trouble and well-rounded.

Even though she'd be tired by sundown, Reece enjoyed all of her daily activities. Never in a million years did she think she'd be living the life of a rich kid. She hardly ever saw Uncle Mason after lunch since he was so busy with his work and keeping his employees in line. She didn't see Jade often either, but that was okay since Jade wasn't very friendly. When Reece wasn't tied up in school or activities, she spent most of her time with Juliet.

Reece's dad came to see her about once a month, but over time his visits became scarce. Uncle Mason would explain that her dad was just having a hard time, especially since they still hadn't found her mother's killer. Perhaps he thought the killers were after him and got Joyce instead. Maybe the murderer was one of dad's jilted lovers. Reece loved her dad and hoped she wouldn't lose the only parent that she had left. Hopefully his burdens wouldn't end up burying him.

Chapter 8

As the years passed, Reece grew to be even more intelligent and prettier than imagined. She was a few months away from her 16th birthday and was a splitting image of her mother, only younger. Her teachers loved her because she was so smart and respectful. The teenage boys adored her, which didn't make her the favorite amongst the female crowd. Reece didn't mind since Juliet was practically her best friend.

As Reece sat down at the breakfast table, she couldn't help but to feel disappointed. It had been almost four months since she had spoken to her dad and a year and some change since she had seen him. No one even mentioned him. She had a feeling that Uncle Mason knew more about her dad than what he led on, but wanted to spare her feelings. Now that Reece was older, she felt as if they could let her in on more things.

"Uncle Mason, since I'm almost sixteen, you do realize that you don't have to hide certain things from me."

"What do you mean?" He asked, almost dropping his fork.

"Well, I haven't heard from my dad in a couple of months. Is he okay?"

"Uh...yeah. He's just out on errands...that's all."

"Oh, okay. You know you can tell me if something is wrong with him, like if he's on drugs or something."

Juliet almost choked on her food. "Reece, why would you say something like that?"

"Because y'all let her say whatever the hell she wanna say." Jade interrupted.

"Here we go." Juliet responded.

"Here we go what? You're supposed to be the girl's mother figure."

"Would anyone like some salt?" Reece asked, antagonizing Jade.

"On a positive note, we have an announcement to make," Uncle Mason said, breaking up the minor quarrel.

"You got my BMW waiting on me outside?"

"Really, Reece," Juliet responded and giggled.

"No, more like an eighty-eight Chevy Cavalier," Mason added.

"Y'all got her spoil like that, so I don't see what the big deal is," Jade stated.

"So what's the big news, Uncle Mason?" Reece asked, ignoring Jade's comment.

Reece was getting fed up with Jade's negative attitude. After discovering what Jade called her daughter's room was a miscarriage that she couldn't get over, Reece stopped respecting anything Jade said. In order to further protect herself, Reece told her uncle what Aunt Patsy had done to her. He made it clear to everyone that any form of punishment for Reece must go through him first. Reece knew that Uncle Mason would never punish her and so did Jade. The tension was constantly building and they both knew it.

"I have just asked Juliet to be my wife." He said.

"We're getting married!" Juliet said, flickering her fingers to show off the ring.

"Oh my god! I'm so happy!" Reece exclaimed, getting up to hug Juliet. "I can't wait to-"

They were all startled by a shattered glass against the wall. All eyes were on Jade who was standing up with both hands on the table.

"Are you fuckin' insane? You have the balls to announce an engagement in front of me! I've been tricking for yo ass since I was seventeen. I'm the one who found this hoe for you. I'm the one who helped you sell your first ten grams and if it wasn't for me, you wouldn't have met Black Eddie. This shit is mad disrespectful! You owe me!"

Juliet was frozen with a horrid look on her face. Uncle Mason was a very humorous and generous person, but he also expected for things to be handled in an orderly fashion. Although Reece hadn't actually seen him discipline any of his workers, she knew Uncle Mason had a low tolerance for bullshit from some of the stories that Juliet had confidently discussed with her.

"Say something dammit!" Jade continued.

No one said anything. Uncle Mason's drug business was definitely new to Reece. She was under the impression that all the money came from his club businesses. It was obviously something that her uncle didn't want her to know, or else he or Juliet would have told her.

"So you...you felt compelled to discuss our private business matters in front of my teenage niece." Uncle Mason said in a disgusted tone after a few minutes of silence.

"Got dammit, she's fifteen! She just said that she's old enough to handle things. She's probably already fuckin' and suckin' just like her mother was. If anything she should be gearing up to be out here with us. And yes, yo daddy is a damn crack addict!"

It was clear to everyone that Jade had taken things too far. Juliet quickly got up and headed towards Reece while Uncle Mason jumped up and slammed Jade on the table by the neck. She squealed in agony as she tried to loosen his stronghold. Juliet hurriedly escorted Reece outside to the pool house. Reece heard Jade scream. The distance wasn't enough to drown out Jade's agonizing screams.

"Reece, I am sorry that this is the way things happened. Never in our wildest nightmares did we expect something like this to come out how it did."

"There's nothing to be sorry about. My mom was a prostitute and my dad is sprung out. Lucky me."

"Reece, that doesn't take away the fact that they loved you and tried to do what was right for you. They really did try hard to give you a different life."

"You know...now that I look back on it, I should've known that my mom wasn't cutting hair for all those hours. The house shouldn't have smelt like that just from cutting hair."

"Reece, I don't know much about your mom, but I do know that some people base their decisions off survival as oppose to what's expected."

"I understand survival of the fittest, but I didn't expect to be lied to by both of my parents."

"Are you okay?"

"No...but I will be. I guess I have to be."

"No matter what, your uncle and I will always take care of you. You're the kid we've always wanted."

The phone rang in the pool house and it was Uncle Mason saying that everything was under control. Once they got back in the dining room, the mess was cleared and breakfast was reset. Jade was also sitting at the table looking downward with her hands in her lap.

"I apologize that I was out of line. I let my emotions get the best of me and I will never disrespect anyone in this house ever again." Jade said as her voice trembled.

"Now...shall we eat," Uncle Mason added as if the entire ordeal didn't just happen.

Even though this was the first time Reece had ever seen a physical altercation in the home, it appeared to be some type of normalcy for them. Jade slowly began to eat her breakfast as Uncle Mason discussed business regarding the club. Every once in a while, Juliet would cut her eyes over at Jade who didn't look up from her plate.

Reece respected the fact that Uncle Mason had no issue with getting his people in line. However, it must have been sheer embarrassment on Jade's behalf. Not because she had gotten disciplined in front of her Uncle's fifteen-year-old niece, but clearly Uncle Mason had made his choice. He chose Juliet.

If everything was true regarding what Jade had said, she didn't stand a chance against Juliet. Perhaps Jade had felt that way but thought if she did more things for him that things would sway in her favor. If there were any doubts before this moment, Uncle Mason had diminished it. Jade was no longer considered a girlfriend. She had involuntarily been reduced to a worker.

Chapter 9

After having the greatest birthday bash ever and being surprised with a new Chevy Camaro, Reece's life couldn't be any better. Uncle Mason and Juliet's wedding was finally here and she couldn't be any happier for them. She still remembered how confused she was when she first heard about Uncle Mason's two girlfriends.

Over the years, Uncle Mason seemed to had gradually become closer to Juliet. Perhaps seeing the way Juliet had taken on the motherly role with his niece made him love her more. He may have even wanted a child of his own. There were rumors going around that Juliet was pregnant, which was presumed to be the reason for the rushed wedding. However, Uncle Mason told her to never believe anything that hadn't come directly from him.

Instead if having the wedding at home, Uncle Mason decided to rent out a Mansion about 30 miles East of Kansas City. It came fully furnished with the wedding decorations, food, and reserved rooms for several of Uncle Mason's special guests. Everything that they could possibly ask for was there including an enormous ballroom with a large outside patio for the reception.

Uncle Mason had refused the Mansion's fully staffed security. He said he didn't want his guest to feel as if they couldn't relax and let loose. The owner stated it was policy to have some of them there whenever there were more than a hundred people occupying the building. The owner assured him that they would remain in their headquarters unless a problem ensued. Much to his resistance, Uncle Mason accepted the terms.

"Reece, could you come here for a second," Juliet called down from her dressing room. "I need you to help me with this tiara."

"Oh my gosh! You are beyond beautiful!" Reece exclaimed as she walked into the room.

"Aww...Thank you. You look like a doll yourself in that maid of honor dress."

"I know, right," Reece smirked, looking in the mirror at her booty.

Juliet laughed. "Girl, you are a mess like your uncle."

"So....where is Jade?" Reece asked.

"Oh, uh...she went to handle some business for your uncle."

"Are you serious? You guys sent her out for business on your wedding day?"

"Reece, no matter what day it is, business is business. Your uncle and I can't do it because we're here."

"But Jewels, you saw how salty she was about everything. I wouldn't trust her for shit. You should have sent me!"

"Language." Juliet warned. "We've been doing this for years. What we do is how she eats. She just had a little outburst that was understandable and discussed. Besides, that was months ago. She's apologized and congratulated us."

"Who's convinced?"

"Who's overstepping their boundaries right now?"

"Seriously, Jewels? You know I'm gonna always look out for y'all. I'm just saying sending someone out to do business on a day they despise is risky."

"Reece, if that's the case, any day is risky."

"My point exactly."

"Hey, let us handle the grown up stuff. Besides, your uncle would kill me if he knew I let you go on runs with me. It's all good. Now stop drooling over yourself and get over here and help me."

"Have you guys heard from my dad?"

"Uh...I haven't. I don't think your uncle has either."

"Oh."

"Tell you what," Juliet started, noticing Reece's sudden sadness, "how about I sneak my favorite girl a glass of Moët at the reception," Juliet suggested.

"How about two glasses?" Reece countered.

"Hey, hey, hey. Don't push it."

A few hours later Reece stood outside next to Juliet in her beautiful off the shoulders, off white gown with her elegant laced veil that matched her train. There was no second guessing as to why Uncle Mason had chosen such a fabulous bride. She was smart, loyal, and simply stunning. You could literally see people's jaw drop when she had walked down the aisle. This had to be the moment that made everything worth it. After a brief exchange of vows and placement of the rings, they were pronounced Mr. and Mrs. Jones.

"Hey, Reece, get over here. I have someone that I want you to meet," Juliet yelled.

The reception was packed with people who weren't at the wedding. Uncle Mason had made it clear that he only wanted their closest friends and family at the actual ceremony. However, the reception was a different story. The ballroom was filled with his strippers from his clubs who were all dressed in nice attire, doctors, lawyers, housekeepers, chefs, and hundreds of others.

"Reece, I would like you to meet my godson, Jeremiah."

"Nice to meet you, Jeremiah. I've never seen you around before," Reece said.

"Yeah, since we moved to St. Louis a few years ago, I hadn't had a chance to come down much." Jeremiah explained.

"Perhaps we can talk your mom into letting you stay with us after your graduation. It would be just like all old times."

"Mr. Over Protective is not going to let a guy my age stay in our house," Reece joked.

"Reece, this is no ordinary young man. He of all people understands the concept of hands off the merchandise."

"Uncle Mason is not cutting my hands off and mailing them to my mom," he said, not seeming to be fully joking.

The more he spoke, the more Reece became intrigued by his demeanor. Not only was Jeremiah very handsome, he was well-spoken and respectful. He didn't focus on her body like most teenage boys and grown men did. He looked straight into her eyes and smiled with those gorgeous dimples. He reminded her of Usher with a little more weight.

"What's up, Jeremiah. Good to see you boy," Uncle Mason said as he walked over, grabbing Jeremiah for a hug. "I see you've met my niece. I'm okay with long hellos but better with quick goodbyes," he joked.

"Don't worry, Uncle Mason. I see her as nothing more or less than a sister."

"God I love this kid."

They all continued to talk and enjoy the fruits of the occasion. Everyone was having an amazing time. Uncle Mason didn't even notice Juliet pass Reece a glass of champagne. They both laughed as Reece glanced at the ballroom floor. Suddenly, she couldn't believe her eyes as she quickly put down her glass.

"Dad?"

Chapter 10

"What did you say?" Juliet asked.

"I think I see my dad."

"Reece, keep it down." Juliet whispered. "Your uncle can't find out about me giving you a drink."

"No, silly. I see my dad! Thank you guys," Reece said, speedily hopping up from the table.

Reece felt as if this was the best surprise ever. She couldn't believe that they had actually gotten a hold of her dad. She now realized why her uncle and Juliet were purposely not speaking of him.

"Uh...Reece...wait!" Juliet said, trying to go after her.

"Shit!" Uncle Mason added, following behind them.

Reece had already dashed toward the ballroom to break through the crowd. There were so many people there that she had a hard time finding her dad. *Wait? Did Uncle Mason say 'shit'?* she wondered. *Why would he be upset that his brother is here*? Then she thought that she may have wasted her drink on the table since she had left so fast.

Reece didn't bother to go back and check. She knew that Juliet and Uncle Mason would understand her excitement. Hopefully, she didn't get the drink on their clothes, but they would have to understand that, too. At this point, it had almost been two years since she had seen her dad. He had missed her last two birthdays, including her sweet sixteen. Although she was happy to see him, he had a lot of questions to answers.

"Daddy!" She exclaimed, after finally finding him. She was halted by what she saw. "Uh...dad?"

"Go ahead and bend dat ass ova and show me something." Bobby was heard saying to one of the club strippers as Reece approached.

Reece's happiness quickly faded. He looked and smelled awful. People in the room had begun to look at him with disgust. Who was this person? This couldn't be the man that she called dad. It was a very awkward moment.

"Oh, uh...hey, baby girl." He said, turning towards Reece. "I was just teasing these strippers. Don't mind me. Where's that big head uncle of yours?"

"What the hell is wrong with you?" Reece asked in confusion.

"Come on y'all. Let's go out into the hallway," Uncle Mason said in a stern voice, gathering her, Juliet, and her dad out of the ballroom. "Everyone please continue to drink and dance," he added, closing the doors.

"What the hell are you doing here!" Juliet screamed.

"Calm down, woman. I'm just here to collect." Bobby responded.

"Your junky ass ain't collecting shit."

"Whoa, Jewels. Don't talk to my daddy like that."

"Yeah, that's right. You tell her, baby girl."

"You need to leave. NOW!" Juliet demanded.

"Okay, everyone be quiet! Bo, why are you here?" Mason asked.

"I'm here for the celebration, bro. What? I can't come to my own brother's wedding plans?"

"He's higher than a damn moon rocket. I'm getting security."

"No, Juliet. Stop." Mason paused, turning back to Bobby.

"Yeah, ain't no need in all of dat, Julia...Juliet. Romeo and Juliet." He stammered, laughing at himself.

"Bo, this is not the time and you should leave," Mason stated, pointing towards the exit.

"Okay, okay, okay. Well, jus lemme get two hundred dollas til tomorrow, bro."

"Bo, you know that's not gonna happen. Call me in the morning when you've sobered up, so we can talk about some things, okay?"

"Okay, well look...I just need the money you getting off my baby girl and that's it. I will be out of yo hair and you guys can go back to your little hoedown. Get it? Hoedown." He said, breaking down laughing this time.

"Listen here you fuckin' low life, cigarette-butt, smelling ass fool. I would neva pimp out my niece. This is like my daughter. Hell, she is my daughter!"

"And I guess the hoe you married is like a house wife, too," Bobby continued, laughing even harder.

"You fuckin' scum!" Mason yelled, lunging at his brother.

"Uncle Mason, wait!" Reece pleaded, trying to grab her uncle's arm that held the tighten grip of his hands around Bobby's neck.

"Come on, Bobby. We don't need this."

Everyone stood in shock by the woman who had approached them from around the corner. Juliet stood still while Reece stared like a deer in headlights. Mason instantly dropped his hands and stepped away from his brother in disbelief.

"Oh my gosh, Bo." Uncle Mason stated, deeply sighing while putting his hand over his eyes.

Juliet tried to grab Reece's arm, but she quickly snatched it away from her. Reece blinked her eyes as if the scene before her would change. She took a step forward, but Uncle Mason used his body as a barrier between the ladies.

"Why...the hell...is Aunt Patsy here?" Reece asked as her voice trembled.

Chapter 11

No one said a word. Tears had begun to form in Reece's eyes. Her stomach began to turn as she remembered the anguish that this woman had caused her at the time of her mother's death. The beatings, the starvation, and the emotional abuse began to flood her memories.

"I thought I told yo crackhead ass to stay in the damn car," Bobby fussed, pushing Patsy back.

"I told you not to take too long or I'm coming in," she argued back.

They stood there arguing back and forth as if they were the only two there. Reece knew what junkies looked like, but this scene rocked her world. She couldn't get past the fact that her dad was with this woman who not only tortured her, but was still her mom's sister. She was aware that her cousin was also her half brother, but Uncle Mason had explained that it was an unplanned situation that happened way before her mom. This questioned everything.

"WHAT THE HELL IS SHE DOING HERE!" Reece screamed as if she was possessed.

Her dad ducked as if someone was going to throw something. "Whoa…young lady, you watch your tone," he said after realizing it was Reece.

"Bobby, what the hell is she doing here?" Reece repeated.

"Bobby? Bobby? Since when did you start calling me Bobby?"

"Well geesh...I don't know. How about when mom died and you stopped being my fucking dad. Now answer my question. Why is this evil bitch here?"

"Bo, why would you bring Patsy here knowing that your daughter was here?" Mason asked.

"Oh. Oh. So everybody wanna make me the bad guy, huh? You've been serving us for months now, Mason. Your own little brother. And now, I'm supposed to be the bad guy, huh? Bullshit."

"Wait. Uncle Mason you knew that my dad was with Patsy?"

"Hell yeah he knew," Bobby bragged, grabbing his crotch while marching in place.

"How could you?" Reece asked, turning her attention back to her dad as her voice cracked and tears fell. "That is my mom's sister, who beat me and starved me by the way. But somehow you picked her out of all women in the world! You said she was dead to us!"

"He was with me first. Your mother just had to have everything that I had," Patsy intervened.

"Bo...man... I have to admit that this is probably the most selfish shit you've ever done," Mason added.

"Oh! Oh! Oh! I'm selfish, huh? You...you got a gang of naked hoes running in and out ya house and I'm selfish, huh?"

Reece leaned back toward the wall and slowly sat down. It was all too much to take in as she placed her head inside her folded arms and continued to cry. She couldn't stop herself from thinking the unthinkable. *Did these two people have something to do with her mom's murder?*

"You two need to leave the premises right now and I'm not fucking playing with y'all," Mason threatened.

"Babydoll," Bobby began, after observing Reece's hurt, "I love you, Babydoll."

"Leave!" Juliet demanded while pointing towards the door.

"Come on, Bobby," Patsy insisted, pulling the tail end of his plaid shirt.

Perhaps the full effects of the drugs were wearing off or a slight sense of dignity had overcome Bobby. "Yeah...alright. I'll leave. But you still owe me," he added, pointing at Mason.

With hesitation, Bobby looked at Reece and turned his head. He slowly walked down the hall with his face towards the ceiling. It wasn't long before you could hear him yelling at Patsy again.

"Reece, do you want to wait out here for a minute or go home?"

"No, Uncle Mason. I'll be fine. You two go ahead and enjoy your reception. I'll get myself together out here."

After reassuring them that she was okay, Uncle Mason helped her up as they both gave her a hug before returning to the ballroom. Reece suddenly felt a cold chill as she stood alone in the hallway. Seeing her dad high out of his mind was crazy, but not as crazy as seeing him with Patsy. Perhaps Uncle Mason had ordered her dad to stay away from her. Although she understood her uncle's intentions, she still would have liked to be informed.

A few minutes later, Reece was interrupted by the opening of the ballroom door. She braced herself as she waited for Uncle Mason or Juliet to further explain the situation regarding her dad. Surprisingly, it wasn't either of them.

"Hey, are you okay?" Jeremiah asked.

"Yeah, just... family stuff," Reece explained while wiping her face.

"Yeah...being raised by Uncle Mason isn't easy."

"What do you mean being raised by him?"

"Well, my mom and I stayed in one of his houses until I was about fourteen. Things were a lot hectic back then, but he always made sure we were good. Uncle Mason stepped in and made sure I kept my head on straight."

"Was your mom also one of his girlfriends?"

"She wasn't to my knowledge." Jeremiah quickly responded.

"Oh, I'm sorry. I just figured-"

"Oh, it's okay. It's a reasonable assumption."

"That's good because that wasn't my intention."

"If you would like, there is a private balcony on the second floor across from the ballroom. We can go there and talk if you needed a minute from the crowd."

Reece agreed as she allowed him to escort her to the secluded area. They waved at Juliet from across the way to make her aware of their whereabouts. Jeremiah was so funny and charismatic that Reece didn't think about what just happened. She was back to enjoying the night with her new acquaintance.

It wasn't long before the night had passed and guest began to disperse from the party. Jeremiah and his mom had a guest room at the mansion, so he continued to keep Reece company. Uncle Mason gave them a sign of approval as he walked off the empty ballroom patio. A few minutes later, a thunderous sound erupted from the parking lot. A sudden blast of light soon followed. It didn't take long for them to realize it was an explosion.

Chapter 12

Reece hurriedly ran downstairs toward the side of the mansion where Uncle Mason had parked. She heard the security guard call for backup as he locked the side door before she could approach it. Reece figured the other guard was at the front or back, so she ran through the ballroom toward the patio. Jeremiah followed close behind as they ran around the mansion toward the commotion.

People were already gathering in hopes to catch a glimpse of what was happening. Along with the darkness, the thick smoke had made it hard to see anything. It would be hard for someone to help even if they tried.

"Alright, everybody get back!" Yelled one of Uncle Mason's business partners.

He and another buff guy kept the crowd at a safe distance away from the flames. Only a few of the extra guests had lingered besides those who were staying for the night. There were about twelve cars on the lot, so it was hard to tell whose car was on fire at first sight. Reece scoured the area with her eyes, but she did not see Juliet or her uncle within the crowd. By this time, smoke had smothered the night air as the blaze continued to roar.

"Where's Uncle Mason?" Reece asked, intending the question for anyone listening.

Jeremiah couldn't answer and anyone else who may have heard her was too focused on the blaze. A security guard ran out the side door with a fire extinguisher and attempted to fight the flames. It was clearly no match for the inferno. However, he tried to focus on the area of the car near the gas tank in order to prevent a massive explosion.

"Oh my God!" He yelled. "Oh my God! It looks like there are people in here! Everybody back up now!"

As the crowd shifted a few steps back, all you could hear was gasping and a few individuals screaming for someone to do something. The truth of the matter was, no one could do anything at this point. The individuals in that car fate had been sealed. A prayer was the only thing left to give.

Reece felt her legs buckle as the weight from her upper body began to overload from her mental imagery. She immediately fell to her knees at the thought of her uncle being trapped in the fire. Jeremiah tried to pick her up and reassure her that it wasn't her uncle, but Reece was in a trancelike state. Losing her uncle would be yet another devastating blow to her already complicated life.

"Reece! Where are you?"

Reece stood up, but she couldn't tell or see who it was calling for her, but it sounded like Juliet. She waited a moment to see if someone would appear. Surely Uncle Mason and Juliet would be together looking for her, but she only heard one voice.

"Reece!" A few seconds later Jade appeared in front of them out of breath. "Didn't you hear me calling after you?"

Reece looked past Jade in hopes that Juliet was behind her. She couldn't hide her disdain for this woman, not even in a crisis. Besides, why was Jade looking for her? Shouldn't she be asking where Uncle Mason and Juliet was?

"Oh, hey Jeremiah! I didn't know you were here. I haven't seen you in ages." Jade mentioned, reaching out for a hug.

"Yeah. I've been here the whole time. You didn't see me at the ceremony?" Jeremiah asked, opting for a handshake instead.

"Well...I guess I got caught up in some grown folks business, so I was running a little late," she smugly responded, embarrassed by his rejection.

"Gosh, I hate that you missed it. Juliet looked so stunning in her gown and Uncle Mason was dressed like a king. Perhaps you'll get to see the hundreds of glamorous pictures that they took together as a newly wedded couple," Reece said, smiling during the entire speech.

Reece knew just how to get under Jade's skin. There was no way in hell that she was going to believe that Jade accidentally missed the wedding. She detested the marriage from day one. Reece was more surprised that Jade hadn't found a way to ruin it.

"Some kids never learn until it's too late," Jade hissed.

"Whatever. Have you seen my uncle and Juliet?"

"You'd be the last to know if I had," mocked Jade, stepping closer to Reece.

"You need to back up, Jade."

"And what are you going to do if I don't, little girl?"

"Whoa, Jade." Jeremiah said, swiftly coming to Reece's aid. "This is a serious situation. They said there were people in that fire, so it has to be someone Uncle Mason knows. Do you mind showing a little respect and courteousness considering the circumstances?"

"Oh, I get it. So now you're captain save-a-hoe. Do you remember when I used to beat your little ass?"

"Well, Jade. Some things are obvious like the fact that I ain't little anymore," Jeremiah added, standing between the ladies, which made him appear that much bigger.

"Find them y'all damn self," Jade said, walking off, not wanting to challenge the young man.

"Forget her. Let's go see what we can find out," Jeremiah stated as he grabbed Reece's hand.

Reece was feeling very perplexed. On one hand, she just witnessed this beautiful wedding, and then she finds out that her dad is a crackhead who is courting her evil aunt that tortured her. To make matters worse, a car is on fire and she can't find her uncle and aunt. On the other hand, she meets Jeremiah who seems to put her mind at ease. Aside from him being attractive and intelligent, she loved how he instinctively inserted himself between her and Jade.

Reece and Jeremiah went back into the mansion to see if anyone else had an update. They made it to the front entrance where they saw a crowd of people surrounding something or someone. Reece slowly maneuvered between the crowd as she spotted her uncle leaning on Juliet's shoulder.

"Oh my God! Uncle Mason! Juliet! You're okay!" She screamed, giving them a tight hug.

"You guys, I've been worried sick—"

Reece stopped in mid sentence. She looked at Uncle Mason and Juliet's faces and hands that were covered in soot from the fire. Uncle Mason felt hot and his clothes were slightly torn and burned.

"Why is everyone just standing around? Where's the ambulance?" Reece yelled, feeling scared and confused. "Are you guys okay? Did you get burned? What happened?"

Uncle Mason and Juliet both turned their heads as Juliet let out an agonizing cry. Reece still didn't understand what had transpired. To her, it appeared as if Uncle Mason and Juliet had gotten away from the explosion in the nick of time.

"We tried!" Uncle Mason cried, bending down to his knees. "We tried."

"What is he talking about?" Reece asked Juliet.

"Reece... let's go talk," Juliet stammered.

"No!" She yelled, turning her attention back to her uncle. "Uncle Mason, I don't understand what's going on, but you're scaring me."

Uncle Mason finally brought himself to his feet. He attempted to wipe his tears, but more flooded his face soon after. He looked at Juliet and held out his hand. Juliet took his hand, slowly walked over to Reece, and grabbed her hand.

"Reece...Reece." Uncle Mason struggled, trying to get his words out. "Your dad was trying to steal my car and—" He couldn't finish. He turned towards Juliet and sobbed even harder.

"No! No!" Reece screamed. "There's gotta be a mistake! It couldn't be him."

Reece waited for her uncle to turn around and agree that maybe it was a mistake. She wanted him to say that he couldn't be a hundred percent sure, so there was still a chance it was someone else. She wanted him to say something. Anything. Except for what he had said.

Deep down inside, Reece knew that it was all real. She'd never seen or even heard of her uncle crying. Her spirit began to weaken as she dropped down to her knees. A faint plea escaped from her lips. "Please tell me it's not true."

Chapter 13

Reece, Juliet, and Uncle Mason all sat down in a small conference room at the mansion with a detective. After crying for hours, Reece was drained once she found out what happened. According to the only two security cameras that were working, Bobby and Patsy never left the premises. They actually mingled with a few guests that were outside on the front patio. Although there were no cameras pointing towards the parking lot, the camera on the right side of the mansion showed Bobby and Patsy creeping in the direction of the cars. Uncle Mason had been notified by a guest that someone was trying to get into his car. By the time he made it outside, his car exploded.

"So...you're saying that you had no idea you had explosives in your car?" The Officer questioned, closing the door and carelessly tossing the report on the table.

"Look, man. I don't have anything else to say but to find the dirt bag that killed my brother and tried to kill me and my wife."

"Mr. Jones, that's exactly what we're trying to do. Now, I spoke with a few guests that claimed your brother was angry and belligerent at the party."

"First off... none of my people would tell you that because we don't have any reason to entertain cops. Second off... I didn't have a damn party. I had a wedding reception. You're married, right officer? You do know what a wedding reception is, correct?"

"Yeah, but all I'm saying is that if your brother pissed someone off at the party or dance or whatever, they may have had a reason to want to see him dead."

"Oh? You mean like the way you're insulting me and pissing me off right now?"

"Hey! I suggest you watch what comes out of your mouth, bud. Look, I'm not the enemy here."

"Are you sure you're not my nemesis, Officer? My brother was just murdered in front of me and you're asking me about someone else's perception of him at what you're refusing to acknowledge as one of the most important days in my life."

"It's not like that at all, Mr. Jones. I actually golf with some of the people on your guest list. The mayor and I just played a game not too long ago down at the country club."

"Is this guy for real?" Mason asked, briefly turning his attention to Juliet. "Look, Officer. I'm not asking for any favoritism. All I want is for you to do your job and get the asshole that did this before I do."

"Whoa, Mr. Jones. You are crossing some serious lines here. Let's not make any threats toward anyone and make a bigger mess than this already is, okay?"

"Officer," Uncle Mason stated, getting up from the table, motioning the ladies to join him while walking towards the door, "that wasn't a threat. That was a promise. You'll be hearing from my lawyer going forward."

"Since the bodies were burned to a crisp, we'll do an autopsy to confirm it was your brother and give it to your lawyer," the officer yelled behind them.

"I hope he gets hit by a fire truck on the way home," Reece mumbled.

A few days had gone by and it seemed as if everyone was still on the edge as they sat at the breakfast table twiddling with their food. Uncle Mason was still paranoid, trying to figure out who set the bomb up in his car. He thought it could have literally been anyone since the word traveled quickly about his marriage by way of the strip club. All he could do was repeat 'how could someone be so vicious and risky' every time there was a discussion.

Reece, however, was more on the edge than anyone. Her mother and father were now both murdered by an unknown assailant. Even though her aunt treated her like shit, she was still family by blood, which made her an additional family victim.

As Reece sat there, her emotions began to fill with rage. What pissed her off even more was the fact that Jade had barely been around since the death of her dad and Patsy was announced and no one thought to question her. Jade acted as if everything was normal. *Uncle Mason and Jewels are both being stupid and naive*, she thought as she glanced back and forth at them. They were so bogged down by their own thoughts that they didn't even notice her intense staring. Enough was enough. Reece was done sitting back allowing the elephant to dance all over the got damn floor.

"Sooo...everyone is just going to sit at this damn table as if shit doesn't need to be addressed?" Reece finally blurted out, unable to mask her aggression.

Juliet was startled and slightly confused by the outburst. No one had literally said anything to one another the entire morning. Juliet looked over at Mason who also had looked up from his plate with raised eyebrows. He didn't say anything. It was as if he knew this moment would come.

"We're all sitting here as if we don't know Jade had something to do with this." Reece continued.

"Reece, I get it. You're upset. You've lost more than a lot and I won't began to imagine how you feel. But you can't blame someone just because you don't get along with them," Uncle Mason reasoned.

"Huh? You think I'm blaming her just because? How about the fact she didn't want y'all married? How bout the fact she happened to miss the entire wedding? What about her absence now? She wasn't looking for you guys during the fire because she was hoping that it was you in the fire!" Reece argued, tearing up with emotion.

Uncle Mason didn't mumble a word. After giving Reece a minute of an empty stare, he looked over at Juliet who also stared blankly at the table. He looked back at Reece who was clearly waiting on a response. He looked back at his plate and said nothing.

"Fine! You guys can stay here while she's in and out, plotting up on her next attack, but I'm not going to sit and wait around!" She yelled, storming off from the table.

Reece entered her room and slammed the door before diving on her bed. Adults are supposed to be so much fucking wiser, she thought. Wiping the hot tears on her cheeks, she got up and paced around the room. She was obviously too young to stay at a motel and all of her Uncle's properties were probably being used for turning tricks. Reece sat on her armchair as she tried to think about other alternatives.

The more Reece's idle mind continued to ponder; anger and resentment had begun to build. She recalled her last encounter with her dad. Even in his drug raging rant, he acknowledged that he loved her. He was clearly sick, but he didn't deserve to die. She loved her dad, just as much as she loved Uncle Mason, who was all she felt she had left besides Juliet. The attempt to kill off her family had to come to an end. Anyone who became a threat to what little family she had left had to die. Starting with Jade.

Chapter 14

"Listen, Reece. I couldn't begin to imagine how you feel. You've been through more than most people will ever go through in a lifetime. I just don't think that this is the right decision to make," Jeremiah reasoned.

"Jeremiah, I'm not asking you to get your nice little hands dirty. All I'm asking you is to get me that thing I asked you for and I'll take care of the rest."

"Don't talk to me like I'm soft. Besides, have you ever even used one before?"

"Yes, I have. Uncle Mason showed me when I was ten."

"Uh huh. So...how do you think he will feel if he knew about this?"

"He'll feel damn good knowing that he will have the ability to take another breath."

"Look, I can't discuss this with you over the phone. Why don't we meet up and have lunch or something."

"Sure, you owe me lunch anyway since you lost that bet."

Reece and Jeremiah had gotten close over the last few months. They talked on the phone everyday and he came to visit almost every other weekend. After Jeremiah's graduation, he decided to temporarily stay in Kansas City. Uncle Mason was fine with it since he considered Jeremiah as his nephew and he knew that Reece could use a friend around her age. He even allowed Jeremiah to stay in one of his apartments.

Reece arrived at the apartment in a lime green tank top with matching confetti shorts. Her soft, fluffy curls were fixed in a loose bun and her multi-colored earrings and bracelet tied her outfit together. The summer heat had given her skin a golden bronze hue that complimented her highlighted hair.

Jeremiah opened the door, embracing her with a one-armed hug as the smell of his lightly scented cologne tantalized her senses. Although she wouldn't admit it, she had developed a small crush on Jeremiah. The fact that he still hadn't ever made a move on her made her that much more interested.

"Wow! That was quick. You must've been doing about ninety all the way over here," he joked, walking towards the back.

"No, I'm just hungry and since lunch is on you, that makes it even better."

Reece glanced around the living room and conjoined kitchen, noticing how he always kept the apartment nice and kempt. Considering that he was a guy, she expected to see snacks, clothes, or even perhaps a few items left by his female friends lying around the place. Come to think of it, he never said if he had a girlfriend or not. She assumed that he didn't since he always seemed to be available for her.

"Lunch is always on me," he said, returning to the front room while grabbing his keys and opening the door for her.

It wasn't long before they arrived at "The Roadhouse" and had gotten settled at their table. They had ordered their drinks and an appetizer as Reece noticed Jeremiah giggle as he texted someone. Right as she was about to ask him what was he giggling about, her attention was then stolen by the laughter of a little girl in the lobby who was twirling under her daddy's arm. It instantly brought back memories of all the fun things her dad once did with her when her mother was alive. It was hard to hold back the tears.

"I want her dead," Reece said softly to Jeremiah.

Aware of their previous conversation, he looked around to see if they were isolated enough before responding. "Reece, getting revenge on her will not bring back your dad. Besides, you're not one hundred percent sure she did it."

"I know she did. I can feel it in my soul. I told you how she acted when Uncle Mason announced his engagement and you saw for yourself how she acted during the fire."

"Reece, that's still not proof. You know what Uncle Mason does for a living. It could have been anyone. He goes crazy when he loses his temper."

"This is what I'm telling you. He lost his temper on Jade a few months back. He slammed her down on the table in front of me."

"Reece," he started and paused, again being distracted by his phone. "Reece, you have to have more evidence than that."

"But I've caught her eavesdropping by Uncle Mason and Juliet's business door."

"Okay, Reece. Let's just pretend that you're right. You do realize that what you want to do is a life changing ordeal, right? There's no coming back from it. You'll live the rest of your life paranoid, thinking that karma will eventually get you."

Reece grew quiet. Although she didn't intend on getting caught, her initial thoughts were that she'd be charged as a minor in a worse case scenario situation. There was no way that she'd get tried as an adult after all she had been through. However, Jeremiah put a different spin on things. He was talking about her actions coming back to haunt her. Did he not realize she'd already been plagued by death? Of course he didn't. He was too busy with his damn phone.

"Maybe if whoever you're giggling with didn't have you occupied you'd take me seriously."

Jeremiah looked up, noticing the change in her tone. "My phone doesn't have anything to do with me trying to make you think rationally."

"Anytime a horny boy thinks about sex it's obvious that nothing else matter."

"Who said anything about sex? Where is this coming from?"

"You're out with me, but you're sexting some bitch."

"First off, you have no idea who is on my phone."

"Well, I hope a dude doesn't have you giggling that way."

"Who do you think you are? You're not my girlfriend. This isn't even a real date. Furthermore, calling someone a bitch that you don't know shows your immaturity. I don't get down with immature girls."

Reece didn't say anything. She politely got up from the table and went to the bathroom in order to calm herself. "Fucking asshole!" She growled as she clenched her teeth. She called Juliet to see if she would pick her up, but Juliet didn't answer. Then, she tried Uncle Mason who also didn't answer. *They're probably screwing or something,* she thought.

Reece took another minute before walking back into the dining room. Jeremiah was right. She wasn't his girlfriend. He hadn't shown her anything different or led her on, but the way he said it was hurtful. A part of her felt rejected and as if she didn't matter to him. She was in her feelings because she had literally gotten too much in her feelings. Now embarrassed, the only thing she thought left to do was ask him to take her back to her car.

"Reece, I didn't mean any harm by what I said." Jeremiah explained as Reece returned to the table.

"It's okay. You said what you said and now we can leave."

"But we haven't even eaten yet."

"You can do whatever you like with me out of your business and out of the picture," she responded, still standing with her arms folded.

Jeremiah couldn't help but to briefly gaze at the cold glare on Reece's face. He let out a deep sigh as he slowly rose from the table. He put two dollars under their drinks and followed Reece out to the car. The ride home was silent as Reece looked out the window as if she'd lost her best friend. In retrospect, she had. There was no way she was ever reaching out to Jeremiah again. This was their end.

"It's not that serious." Jeremiah said, stopping at the red light a few blocks away from the apartment. "I felt disrespected by how you came at me, so I reacted. Forgive me if my words were harsh."

Reece didn't respond. There was no need. He made it clear that he wasn't interested in her. There wasn't much else to say.

"Reece, we're best friends. You can't ignore me forever."

Just as Reece was considering a sarcastic response, she received an incoming call. She looked down at her phone, noticing it was Juliet. It was too late for Juliet to come pick her up at this point, so she allowed the call to go to voicemail. However, Juliet called right back. Reece immediately knew something wasn't right. Juliet never called twice in a row. Calling someone back to back was a pet peeve of hers.

"Juliet? Are you okay?" Reece quickly asked before Juliet could speak.

"Reece...Reece," Juliet said in a weak tone, "Don't...Don't-"

The line went silent.

Chapter 15

"Jeremiah! We have to turn around right now! Something happened to Juliet and Uncle Mason!" Reece hysterically shouted.

"Reece, calm down. I'm sure everything is fine. What did she say?"

"It's not what she said. It's what she couldn't say. She sounded like she was dying! We gotta go help her!"

"Okay. Let me run in the crib and grab something real fast."

"Jeremiah, we don't have time!"

"Reece, we can't make a U-turn in the middle of this intersection, so we have to pass by the complex anyway. I'll be in and out real fast."

Jeremiah pulled up to the complex and hurriedly got out of the car. What was probably seconds felt like minutes to Reece. She got out of Jeremiah's car, jumped in hers, and sped off from the parking lot.

Reece made it back home in a matter of minutes. She normally parked in the garage, but she figured every minute counted. Without even cutting off her car, she rushed through the front door.

"Juliet? Uncle Mason? Where are you guys?"

The house was unusually silent. No one was in view in the hallways or the living area. It appeared as if even the workers had left. With soft, tiny footsteps, Reece slowly made her way toward the kitchen. Once she rounded the corner where the dining table was, she began to tremble in fear. Uncle Mason was lying in a pool of blood on the floor.

"Oh my God! Uncle Mason! Are you okay?" She yelled, running to his aid.

As soon as she kneeled down to see if he was breathing, she felt cold metal on her shoulder. Although she couldn't see the person who was behind her, Reece had a feeling it was exactly who she had warned them about. She didn't make any sudden moves, but she decided to talk to the person as if she already knew it was Jade. If it wasn't Jade, then perhaps the person would just knock her out and leave, assuming they were in the clear. If it was Jade, then she knew exactly what to say to buy her some time.

"Listen, Jade. I am only sixteen. My mom is gone, my dad is gone, and now I have nothing. I've been secretly wanting to die for a while now. But...about a week ago, I found out that I was pregnant. It made me feel like I had a reason to live again. You were right. I mean...I'm not a whore...but I'm not as innocent as I led Uncle Mason and Juliet to believe."

"I knew it. I fucking knew it," Jade proclaimed, kicking Reece over on the floor to face her. "You've been a little sneaky slut this whole time. You don't deserve to have a child," Jade continued, with the gun still pointed toward Reece's face.

"Jade, you know I lost my mom when I was a little girl. This is a miracle of love for the both of us. My mom's spirit of love brought this baby to me," Reece pleaded, forcing tears to make her lie more believable.

"Ha! Your mom's spirit of love? Reece...let me tell you a few things about your whorish mom, may she rest in hell. She got murdered because she couldn't keep her legs closed. What? Don't look at me like that. It's the truth. Your dad found an open condom wrapper in a man's wallet under his couch."

Reece gasped in horror. What in the hell was going on? How did Jade know about that wallet?

"Wait. How...who...?"

"How did I know that? Well, little-grown girl, I have more juicy facts for you. Unbeknownst to your dirty uncle, your father and I had been fucking since your mother was pregnant with you. Your father wanted to stay around and raise his little brat, so I allowed him to. The night that your dad found out your whorish mom was cheating, he had the audacity to call me, crying over that horrid trash. I suggested that he choke her out for being disrespectful enough to bring another man in the house where he paid bills and his daughter resided. Hell, I didn't know he'd choke her to death."

"You're a liar! You're an evil, got damn liar with no soul," Reece screamed, her eyes now flooded with tears of hatred. "My dad would never do that! He loved my mom!"

"Reece, your dad was the devil himself. He got your aunt pregnant first, denied the child, moved on to her little sister, and then impregnated her, too. He even convinced me to abort a child. He's a loser that deserved what he got."

"No one deserves to die you sick lunatic!" Reece blurted out, unable to hold in her rage.

"When you fuck with me you do. Your uncle is laying here dead right now because he habitually embarrassed people. He was an asshole and a dictator. Those explosives in his car were clearly for him. Now, had your dumbass dad not messed it up by flaunting your hoe ass aunt in my face, he'd still be around to snort a line. Well...provided if he hadn't overdosed by now."

"You're so screwed up in the head. I knew your evil, pathetic ass had something to do with that."

"Pathetic? No, what was pathetic was how easy it was to convince those two drug addicts to steal your uncle's car. All I had to do was tell them that your uncle got his big time lawyer to give him your mother's death settlement. Boom! He ate it up like a toddler to ice-cream."

"No wonder why no man would wife you. It would be suicide. I hope you burn in hell, bitch."

"Wow! You got some pretty big balls to talk to me like that with this gun in your face. Then again, your family is dead. You don't have anything to lose. You'd probably be a loser mother like your mom. I'd be doing that baby a favor."

"Put the gun down, Jade." Jeremiah demanded, walking around the corner with a fully loaded revolver.

"Oh, shit! Its little Jeremiah. What brings you here? Ohhh! I get it. That's your baby, too. You're a busy little bastard aren't you? Wait. You do know that it is a crime to get a minor pregnant though, right? You're eighteen and she's sixteen."

"What the hell are you talking about? Besides, that didn't stop you from trying to get this wood when I was fifteen now did it, Jade?"

"Fuck you, Jeremiah! You're the little shit that your dad should have squirted into your mom's mouth."

"No, fuck Black Eddie who made you lose those twins. Everyone knew those weren't Uncle Mason's babies. Thought I didn't know about that, huh?"

"You little shit," Jade said, swallowing hard as she began to tear up. "Drop the fucking gun before I blow her head off!"

"I'm not dropping shit. Everyone knows you're the type of woman that can't be trusted. And that my friend…is the reason why you were never chosen."

Jade quickly glanced at Reece and back at Jeremiah. It was almost as if he had snatched the last bit of decency from her soul. As if it was in slow motion, Jade turned and shot at Jeremiah who yelled in agony. Fearing that Jade would go finish him and her off, Reece made a daring move by extending her leg and tripping Jade as she fell to the floor. The gun also fell on the floor a few feet away as both ladies tried to scramble to get it. As much as Reece fought, Jade proved to be stronger than Reece and snatched the gun first. Almost out of breath, she stood over Reece once again.

"I've been waiting for this day for a while now. You've been nothing but a thorn in my side since the day you arrived at our home. Say...say your last prayers slut."

Reece didn't say anything. She took a deep breath and closed her eyes. The first thought that came to her mind was her mother. She remembered how beautiful she was when she smiled. She thought about when she was four and how her mom read to her every night before bed. She also recalled the last time her mother said 'I love you' and hugged her.

Then, the pleasant memories of how her dad bought her tons of dolls and took her to countless playgrounds and ice-cream parlors began to resurface. She smiled. It was at that moment that she realized that they did do all they could for her considering the circumstances. She knew it was going to be okay. Everything happens for a reason. She suddenly became at peace. A few seconds later, shots were fired.

Chapter 16

A loud thump came right after the sound of the pistol rounds. There was a brief silence and then a soft whimper. Reece opened one eye and then the other. She didn't feel anything as she looked down at her body to confirm. She quickly looked forward and saw Jade lying a few feet away with bullet holes in her chest.

"Reece! Are you okay?" Juliet asked, bleeding as she was hurdled over the kitchen island.

"Oh my God, Jewels!" Reece screamed, hurrying to her aid.

Reece helped Juliet to a chair and looked around for her cell phone. Apparently, someone had already called the police because they heard sirens not far from the home. Reece placed a dinner cloth over Juliet's wounds, which was close to her chest. After elevating her feet, she grabbed Juliet's hand and told her to hold it there while she checked on Jeremiah.

Reece grasped in horror as she saw blood protruding from Jeremiah's head. Not sure if he was dead or not, she ran to the nearest bathroom and grabbed some towels. She placed the towels where the wound was and tied it around his head.

Reece looked over across the room at her uncle who was still lying on the floor. She presumed he was dead since he hadn't moved. Jade had also confirmed he was dead, but Reece never got a chance to see for herself. Just as Reece was about to go and check on Uncle Mason, the police barged through the door.

"Hands up!" The policeman yelled.

"Hands up? What do you mean hands up? My family is dying you bastard!"

"Reece, stay calm. Officer...that...that lady over there...on the floor tried to kill us all," Juliet tried to explain, short of breath. "I shot her. My gun...my gun is on the counter."

It wasn't long before more officers arrived on the scene along with paramedics. They worked on Uncle Mason and Jeremiah until they eventually took them away in an ambulance. Reece was the only one they could get a full statement from after she was escorted to the hospital.

The news of Uncle Mason and Juliet's shooting spread like wild fire. Women from the club, Uncle Mason's business partners, and a few people Reece noticed from the wedding reception came to the hospital. Unfortunate for them, no one was allowed back to see Uncle Mason since he was in critical condition. It seemed as if as soon as the visitors came in, they immediately left.

"Excuse me, Reece?" A nurse walked up and asked.

"Yes, that's me."

"Well...your mother's surgery went well. They're expecting her to have a full recovery. However, the doctors are still operating on your brother as we speak. Your mother is actually awake and stable. Would you like to see her?"

Reece considered correcting the nurse, but figured that she shouldn't. Perhaps being known as the daughter and sister gave her access to everyone. Besides, no one had yet came in and asked for Jeremiah. He was definitely going to need someone by his side. She also noticed that the nurse didn't mention Uncle Mason. She wasn't going to allow her to slip off that easily.

"Hey, nurse. What about my Un...I mean my dad?"

"I'm sorry, Reece. If I can be honest with you, it's not looking good. He lost a lot of blood and-" She stopped, quickly walking down the hall after getting paged.

As much as Reece wanted to cry, she couldn't. She knew she had to be strong for Juliet who'd ask her questions. She took a deep breath and tried to think positive thoughts before walking into the room.

"Hey, Jewels! How are you feeling? I'm so happy to see you awake!" Reece exclaimed, walking over to give her a gentle hug.

"I feel a little better. Getting shot is something I wouldn't wish on anyone. I went from feeling like I was in my early thirties to my late eighties," she lightly chuckled, followed by a cough.

"How did it happen?"

"Your uncle and I had just come back from taking care of a little business in town. We noticed that the gardeners were gone and it was completely silent once we walked in the house. Your uncle immediately got on the phone to call the head housekeeper, and then all of a sudden we heard a loud bang. It was like life had completely stopped."

"Did y'all already know it was her or did she have on a mask or something?"

"She was definitely in a blind spot around the corner because we didn't see anyone. All of a sudden, I heard the weirdest gasping sound ever. It was faint, yet agonizing. I immediately turned towards your uncle who was looking straight forward with glassy eyes. He instantly fell back with his phone still in his hands."

"So...he never got to see who shot him?"

"Not unless he was still conscious and heard her voice. Before I could even get to him Jade stepped forward, pointed the gun towards me and asked me where you were. I thought you were in your room, so I pleaded for her to leave you alone. When you called me, I knew you weren't home. I waited until she went to find you, then..." Juliet paused, mentally recalling the horror.

"That's when you called me and tried to tell me not to come, so she shot you," Reece completed for her, watching tears form in Juliet's eyes as Juliet shook her head in agreement.

"I'm so sorry, Jewels," Reece continued, also beginning to cry.

"What did they say about your uncle?"

Reece knew the question was coming. As strong as Juliet was, Reece knew that she couldn't give Juliet the same information that the nurse had given her. She had to choose her word wisely.

"He's not where they need him to be, but Uncle Mason is still fighting. He always did say that giving up was never an option."

Juliet chuckled. "He did."

Reece figured that this small glimpse of hope was the best time to leave. "Well...uh, I guess you should rest since the nurse keeps looking in here."

"It's not you. She's probably mad because I keep buzzing them for more morphine."

They both laughed as Reece began to exit the room. Before exiting the room, Reece paused. She turned around and looked at Juliet.

"Juliet."

"Yes, love."

"Thank you for being someone you didn't have to be."

Reece was on her way back to the sitting area when she was stopped by a different nurse. They explained that her brother was in very bad shape and he needed someone by his side. The nurse also explained to Reece that this could very much well be his last conversation.

Reece walked into Jeremiah's room not knowing what to expect. He was hooked up to three different machines and had attachments from practically every part of his body. You could still see fresh blood emerging from the wrap around his head.

"Jeremiah, are you woke."

"Reece... Reece," he responded, trying to breathe between his words. "This is...this is horrible. It wasn't supposed to be like this. This wasn't the way it was supposed to happen."

"Keep hanging in there, Jeremiah. Please don't give up. You're my best friend," Reece cried.

"Reece...Reece...it's okay. My mother will be here soon. Tell her...I love her. And since...since you already know about the baby... I'm asking you as my friend to help Juliet raise him right...Tell her...Tell her to make sure that he or she doesn't become the monsters that we were. I never wanted Uncle Mason to die. I didn't. Maybe...maybe this was God's way of letting the good live in peace."

"Uhm...wait. What? I don't understand wha-"

"Promise me, Reece. Just...just take care of the baby."

It was complete silence for a minute. Reece thought that Jeremiah was catching another breath to say something, but he didn't. A few seconds later the machines started to beep like crazy. The nurses rushed in and quickly removed Reece from the room.

"Jeremiah!" She yelled, as tears fell down her cheeks.

Reece watched as more doctors rushed into the room. After the nurses closed the blinds, Reece was escorted back to the main waiting room. *Was any of what Jeremiah said true? Was Juliet really pregnant by him? She didn't even look pregnant. Did Juliet have something to do with this entire setup*? It was one thing to get a mouthful of pure betrayal from someone she considered as her best friend, but for him to die right after that was twice the devastation.

Chapter 17

As Reece sat in the waiting room, Jeremiah's words replayed in her head like a broken record. She thought about Jeremiah's confession versus Juliet's version and what she saw for herself. She had never known Jeremiah to lie to her about anything. He also knew he was dying, so what reason did he have to make up something so extreme on his death bed?

Reece also considered how strange it was when Juliet had told her that they were all in the room together when Jade shot Uncle Mason, but Juliet was no where in site when she and Jeremiah arrived. As a matter of fact, Juliet didn't come out until much later. Had Juliet tricked Uncle Mason into marrying her because of the pregnancy? Uncle Mason certainly wouldn't have married Juliet knowing it was Jeremiah's baby. But if Juliet was in on the conspiracy, how did she get shot? Surely, she wouldn't allow herself to get shot knowing she was pregnant. It was all so confusing.

Now that Reece was finally alone, she couldn't stop the events from swarming in her head. How could she believe a person like Jade? Jade wanted everyone to be as evil as of a person as she was. Her dad wouldn't ever consider messing around with a woman like her, less knowing confide in her.

And then, for Jade to say that her dad killed her mom was really absurd. Her dad loved her mom. As much as he cheated, surely he would have forgiven her mom for one indiscretion. The more Reece thought about it, she realized that her dad really...really loved her mom. *Could it have been a crime of passion*? How else did Jade know about that damn wallet? Reece was extremely baffled. There was something there, but Reece couldn't figure out what it was. She needed answers and she needed them now.

It wasn't long before Reece had slipped back into Juliet's room. It was now the only room she had to sleep in since Jeremiah had passed and Uncle Mason was still hanging on to dear life. Reece assumed that Juliet would be asleep, but she wasn't. She was oddly staring at the wall, looking as if she had made the worst decision of her life. Reece wished that she could read Jade's thoughts.

"Uhm...I guess you heard about Jeremiah since they assumed you were his mother," Reece said, closing the door.

"Yeah…I did. I uh…told them that I wasn't you guys' mother. I also gave the nurse Jeremiah mother's information. She probably didn't know about any of this up until this point. I couldn't even imagine the devastation she'll carry of losing her only child." Juliet responded in a solemn tone.

Reece couldn't tell if she was being sincere or not. Perhaps Jeremiah's death was now convenient. It was clear that Juliet didn't expect that Jeremiah had told her anything about him being the father of her baby. Reece decided that she wasn't going to tell Juliet exactly what he had confessed to her from his death bed, but she wasn't going to beat around the bush either.

"So...why didn't you tell me you were pregnant?"

"Those damn nurses can't keep there mouths closed, huh?"

"So…why were you trying to hide it?" Reece continued, not wanting to confirm or deny the question.

"I...well...we didn't want to jinks it."

"We?" Reece asked.

"Well, your uncle and I had been trying for some time now. We even had a miscarriage a couple of years back, but we've been unsuccessful since. We figured it was karma from all the abortions that we paid for the strippers to have. But thankfully," she continued, beginning to cry, "we finally conceived. You should have seen how his face lit up when I told him. And now, to find out that the shot didn't harm the baby just confirmed this miracle. This is definitely our miracle baby. I'm praying that your uncle pulls through. This is our new life together."

Reece was at a loss. What if Juliet thought that having this baby was the only way to have the family life that she'd dreamed of having? What if she figured that Uncle Mason couldn't produce anymore, so she used Jeremiah to be her sperm donor? If this was the case, wouldn't Juliet have been afraid that Jeremiah would eventually tell the truth? Nah, Uncle Mason was clearly too unpredictable for Jeremiah to do that. And now with Jade and Jeremiah dead, Reece would never know if Juliet was in on it.

"Reece, your uncle is asking for you," a nurse walked in and interrupted.

"Oh my God! Is he conscious? I have to go see him!" Juliet said in excitement.

"Yes, Mrs. Jones, he is conscious, but you must lie back down and get your rest. We can't have you in the ICU in your condition. We've already informed him that we successfully removed the bullet from you and the baby is fine."

Reece could see the worry release from Juliet's face as she closed the door and followed the nurse out of the room. Although Juliet seemed sincere, Reece couldn't tell if it was an act or not. She was clearly a liar and a cheater at this point, but to what measure?

"Hey, Uncle Mason. Are you still woke?" Reece asked Uncle Mason, who was facing away from the door.

"Hell, I guess I am," he said, turning while cracking a small smile. "Are you okay? I heard about Jeremiah. That was a damn good kid."

"Yeah, I guess I have no choice but to be alright. I mean...I'm still a little shook up, but I guess I'm okay."

"A little shook up? After all that you have experienced, I'd be somewhere in an insane asylum if I were your age."

"Yeah...well...a great man once said that no matter how shattered your life seems, you can always find a way to put the pieces back together."

He chuckled, "I remember telling your dad that during his bad times because that's what our grandma always told us. And that's something that I've always admired about you, Reece. You listen, you observe, and you utilize. I'm ashamed to admit that I sometimes envy your passion and ambition."

"Why does it have to take everyone to die in order for me to be this so-called strong person?" Reece asked, not able to fight back the tears. "I'm not that strong."

"Reece...I have no logical explanation for any of this. Me, on the other hand, I've been a savage. I probably deserved this and much more. But not you. I'm sorry, Babydoll, for your loss. Even though you may not see now, God definitely has a plan for you."

Epilogue

Two years later, Reece sat in her graduation chair about to give her speech as valedictorian of her high school class. She received a full scholarship to Spellman University due to her academics and the essay that she wrote about her childhood. She was also praised for her community work for helping young girls cope with tragic situations.

As Reece sat there and looked out amongst the crowd, she saw Juliet holding her baby cousin, Braylon who was already clapping as he stood in her lap. He was so attached to Reece that people had thought that he was her child. Uncle Mason and Juliet were determined for him to have a different lifestyle than what they had. They had sold the strip clubs and stopped all underground activities.

Although life had brought a decent change for Reece the past few years, there were unresolved issues in her mind. From time to time, she thought about how devastated Jeremiah's mom was at the hospital. She literally had no one else, but her son. The cries and screams would haunt Reece forever. It had definitely crossed Reece's mind to let his mother know that her son is living on through her grandson who was also Uncle Mason's son. But Reece knew she couldn't. She couldn't risk anyone else's life.

Reece still wondered did Juliet have something to do with Uncle Mason getting shot. She wondered had Jeremiah lived, if the situation would be different. What if Juliet had fallen in love with Jeremiah, and the plan had been to get rid of Uncle Mason? However, when Jeremiah died, it was only convenient to go with the new circumstances. Perhaps Juliet shot Jade because she didn't want Jade to uncover their plans. There were still so many questions.

Reece had also always wondered did Uncle Mason have any suspicion about baby Braylon being his child, but she never asked. She knew it would change everything. She could possibly get kicked out of their lives and baby Braylon's life had she opened up that conversation. Reece decided it would be up to Juliet to be able to wake up for the rest of her life and live with the fact that she was pretending to have a child by Uncle Mason.

The cool breeze had blown a piece of hair onto the necklace that her dad had bought her the day her mom died. The moment gave Reece the comfort of feeling as if her mom and dad were there in spirit, and that perhaps God had given them both a second chance. She knew that she'd probably never know if her dad killed her mom. At times she wondered had she never kicked the wallet under the couch would her parents still be alive. Whoever did it, she still hoped that God would have mercy on their soul. At this point, she didn't want to know. She decided to collect the broken pieces of her life and create a beautiful masterpiece.

From the Author

"Thank you for taking the time to read Reece in Pieces. I look forward to providing you with future entertainment that you will enjoy."

AND PLEASE...

If you'd like more quality fiction at this low price, I'd really appreciate a review on Amazon. The number of reviews a book accumulates on a daily basis has a direct impact on how it sells, so just leaving a review, no matter how short, helps make it possible for me to continue to do what I do. Here's a link to leave a review. Thank you in advance!

Customer Review

Feel free to check out the entire series as well as other books also available on Amazon.

Partially Broken Never Destroyed Complete Series

We Were Still Kids

The Doctor's Inn: A Private Practice

A Crime for Two

Alyce Leaves Wonderland

After Dawn Breaks

www.imadethebook.com

Unlawful Vows (Sample)

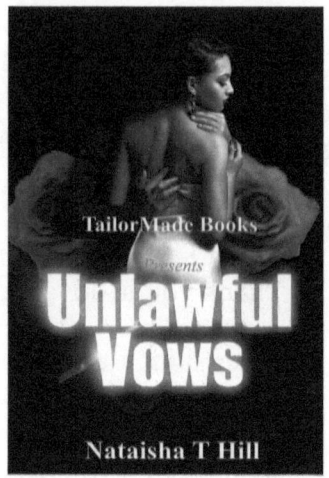

"One less filth in the world," Sandra mumbled as she trembled so hard that it seemed the four walls of the basement were spinning around her. *Or were they?* She couldn't tell. She could only tell of the tremor inside of her. Her heart rocked in her chest, as though she'd been in a death race. She was visibly shaking. If she grasped an object, it would slither from her grasp and crash down into the floor. She was that unsettled.

Her hair, honey brown and wavy, was drenched with the sweat dripping down her caramel skin. If she wasn't stark naked, her clothes would be just as wet as her hair. It had been days since she last felt the comfort of clothes. At least proper ones. Lately, she was forced to go on without clothes, and when 'they' did let her get dressed, they only provided her with clothes that fuelled their sexual perversion. Vulnerability to the harshness of the extreme weather was nothing new to Sandra at this point.

It didn't matter that she'd been forced to forgo her skincare regimen for many weeks at a stretch. Her skin still looked radiant, holding its rich caramel glow. She was the true definition of a diamond in the rough.

Her knees buckled, seeking to give way as she stood on her feet. As if that wasn't enough to drive her back to the floor, there was the painful throbbing between her legs, where the man, her so-called master, had delivered a blow with his clenched fist. Now he lay nude and motionless, his life sucked out of him. His eyes were wide open, yet seeing nothing.

They were the same eyes that had always been brimming with lust and power when he took her, tossing her back and forth like a ragged doll. It was ironic how she'd strangled him with the very same handcuffs he'd restrained her with. *Poor thing*, she thought and smirked. He definitely hadn't seen it coming. If he'd known the chains of the handcuffs would bring him to his death, he certainly would not have introduced the handcuffs into his perverted game two weeks ago.

Sandra waited for the perfect time to strike. She waited for a moment when he approached her alone, with his wife nowhere in sight. Glancing at the dead man, her eyes were frantic to find the key to the handcuffs. Sandra had found it resting on his chest where it doubled as a pendant. She crouched beside him, yanked the key off his neck and unlocked the cuffs. The cuffs fell to the floor, clanking loudly. She bristled. That was way louder than it should be. She could only hope her boss's wife hadn't heard it.

Careful not to make a sound, she advanced toward the exit, but her plan to be silent was defeated when she mounted the stairs leading out of the basement. The wooden stairs, old and rickety, creaked with each step she took. Without the death sting of iron around her wrists, her skin could finally breathe again. *Freedom, Sandra. That's the smell of freedom.*

Sandra breathed deeply, filling her lungs with fresh air. This air was different. It was poles apart from the stuffed air trapped in the basement, or dungeon as she liked to call it. The air in the basement was rather foul, clogged with the smell of rust, sweat and of course…sex—if sex had a smell.

Sandra had no idea what time it was or what day it was. She'd lost track of time. She barely even knew when it was morning or evening, unless her boss approached her with a derogatory greeting on his cigarette-darkened lips.

The house was quiet, as though there was no sign of life. But she had a feeling her mistress was up there in the master's bedroom. She proceeded toward the stairs leading to the bedroom. Cold sweat dripped down her hair and trailed down her spine, until it found her butt crack. The air conditioner had her perspiration drying up in no time though. Her steps were unhurried, almost soundless, as she made her way to the master's bedroom.

She pushed open the door, her eyes straining to see through the darkness of the room. Her eyes adjusted to the darkness—it was nighttime, obviously—and then her gaze settled on a bump on one side of the bed. Sandra smiled. There Marie was, having her beauty sleep.

She lay on her side, her head resting on one of the many soft pillows on the bed. She'd definitely fallen asleep with the thought that her husband was down there in the basement having his way with their sex slave. Sandra edged closer to Marie and then she halted, her eyes devouring the woman.

She had no idea of killing this one. Marie looked…innocent. Naïve even. What if just like Sandra, Marie had also been sexually enslaved to the pervert? What if their marriage was one huge lie and she also needed saving? More questions crowded Sandra's mind, and then she sat beside Marie and touched her arm through the covers under which she lay.

"Mmmh," Marie hummed, adjusting herself on the bed. "Go shower, Carl. You must stink after being in that pathetic place for hours."

Hours? Sandra wondered. This woman was clearly exaggerating. *Was she drugged*? Perhaps she was too far gone in her slumber to think right. Her husband had only been there for a few minutes. Twenty at the most. He clearly had something even more sinister going on outside of them both, but whatever. None of that mattered at the moment.

Marie was silent again. She had obviously drifted back into sleep. Sandra concluded that she'd been right to think that Marie was naïve. Couldn't she feel that her husband was gone? Couldn't she feel that the person beside her wasn't her Carl? Seriously though, couldn't she feel that something had happened to him? Wasn't there a way these people felt these things? Unless of course, the movies and books were all lying. If this was a movie, she'd definitely feel that her husband was gone. Maybe she'd suddenly feel dizzy, or feel a sharp sting or a stab in her chest. Anything.

This woman felt nothing. She lay there without a care in the world, her chest rising and falling gently as she breathed. Sandra couldn't deny that while she hated every moment with Carl, she'd always looked forward to having sex with Marie. In those few months she was locked up in the dungeon, she realized a truth about herself—one she wished she'd known sooner.

She had a soft spot for women. There was a hole in her life that could only be filled by a woman, and Marie looked perfect.

So, she bent toward Marie and kissed her ear. She ran her hand up and down Marie's arm, and then she whispered, "Come with me. Let us leave this place."

Partially Broken Never Destroyed (Sample)

Kayla's peace was short lived when Jeremy called her a week later, saying he wanted to make amends and at least be friends. He talked about the things he had done wrong and realizing the error of his ways. He offered to take her out to a friendly dinner so he could explain some of the things that took place. When she asked him why he couldn't just explain himself over the phone, he claimed that it was important to say what he had to say face-to-face. Who was he kidding? She knew what he was up to as always. His little fling didn't turn out as he expected. Although she had absolutely no intentions of getting back with him, she wanted to hear his reason for cheating.

Jeremy and she agreed to meet at one of their favorite restaurants called Parquet's. She figured she would dress sexy in order to rub in all of what he had been missing. She wore a black, off the shoulders, one-piece pantsuit with her leopard pumps that matched her leopard accessories. She still wasn't exactly sure how much information Jeremy had regarding Travis or any of what had went down. Being that it was a small town and one of his basketball friends was at the party with Richard and her, there was no telling what he knew. She arrived at the restaurant and noticed Jeremy was already there. The host directed her to his table and he was sitting there looking quite handsome with his black, short-sleeved polo shirt and dark blue jeans. He got up from the table and greeted her with a hug.

"Damn, girl, you upgraded since you left me, huh?"

"I left you? Is that how it went?" Kayla jokingly replied.

"No, I'm just talking, so what's new in your life? A new man perhaps?"

"Not really, I'm just taking some time to myself. How are you and your new? "

"What makes you think I have a new?"

"Well, there is the fact that I saw you two together one day and then you confirmed it weeks ago."

"Oh, that was nothing."

"So, you ruined something good over a tasteless female."

"It wasn't that, I was just going through some things with my dad and you and I were arguing all the time, I didn't know what to do."

"So, you figured the answer would be to have sex with another woman?"

"That's sort of what I wanted to talk to you about," he sighed and paused. By that time, the server came by to get their drinks.

"Proceed," she said, sounding a bit urgent.

"That girl claiming she is pregnant."

Kayla sat there in dead silence. She could not believe this loser was sitting here telling her he got someone pregnant. What in the hell was he thinking telling her this? As much as she convinced herself that she didn't want him anymore, knowing that he got someone pregnant burned her inside. She could feel the cruelty in her gradually increasing.

"What are you telling me this for, hell, you should've had her here instead of me since you got an extra person to feed."

"Damn, see that's why I wanted to talk to you face-to-face, because I knew if I did it over the phone, you would have just hung up. At least now I know you still care."

"Have you seriously lost your mind? Lose my number and die," she responded as she got up and left from the table not looking back.

"Kayla," he yelled as she was leaving, "KAYLA!"

She jumped in her car, pissed to the limit. She couldn't believe that whorish guy, who called himself a man, would get some random female pregnant. She started feeling even more justified about having sex with Travis. She started to think about how Jeremy would always say he would marry the woman who carried his first child. Then she started to feel nauseated by the thought that he may really love this woman and treat her right. She really couldn't understand why she was so upset. It's not as if this guy treated her like a queen or something, so why was she sweating this issue. Consumed by her thoughts as she pulled into her apartment complex, she didn't notice someone had been following her. She parked her car only to discover to the right side of her was Jeremy's truck. Jeremy had followed her home.

Panic came over her because she didn't know what to do. She pretended to fondle around in her purse until she could think of a good lie. He pretty much knew where the majority of her relatives lived, so she couldn't say it was an aunt or cousin's home. She was busted. She had practically given this mentally deranged man direction to her home. She decided not to worry since 9-1-1 was just a phone call away if he tried something.

"Oh, so you really came up," he said, as Kayla finally got out of her car.

"Yeah, and?"

"Oh, I'm not hating or anything, congratulations."

"Yeah, thanks," she dryly responded.

"It's good to see you're doing good and not being a low-life like all my other ex-girlfriends. Miss independent and I don't need anything from a man," he teased.

"Look, Jeremy, I don't know why you followed me; I said all I had to say at the restaurant."

"That's cool, are you going to invite me in so I can see how you're living?"

"This isn't the time and, plus, I have to be at work here shortly so…"

"How about I call you tonight and we can talk about it," he interrupted.

At this point, she didn't want him in her home, by any means. All she wanted was to see him leave and never return, so she agreed. Much to her surprise, he got in his truck, without any hesitation, and left. She felt relieved and overwhelmed all at once. She was so upset with herself for not going over to her mom's house or stopping by the store or something before going home. She started to wonder if she should buy a bat or something just in case. She had already been thinking of getting a gun, since she was a single female living on her own. Now that Jeremy knew where she stayed, it really wouldn't be such a bad idea.

At work, things weren't going any better. One of the day shift managers had written her up because she got a guest complaint the night before. The complaint claimed she was too slow bringing the food out and after she brought it out, it was cold. She couldn't help one of their lazy night shift cooks didn't feel like re-cleaning the grill. Then, Brandy had called out from work for some reason, so she figured she would have to listen to Rachael simplistic ass all night. One of the night managers informed her that the usual new hire trainer wouldn't be in, so she wanted her to train the new girl, Dana. It was just like them, to write her up and then need a damn favor.

Dana was a medium built chick with long curly hair and smooth brown skin. She had wide hips and a slightly cute face. Her only drawback was her legs were somewhat short, accentuating her too long torso. Kayla discovered that Dana dated one of her cousins back in the day, so the conversation they had while she was training her didn't seem awkward. Kayla told her she should come out with her and Brandy sometimes. Dana promptly accepted her offer. This was cool for Kayla, since her and Dana were single while Brandy was spending more time with her man.

It wasn't too long before Kayla ended her shift when Jeremy called. Just seeing his number on her cell phone made her cringe. She decided not to answer since she seriously didn't feel like dealing with him. Just as she pulled around the corner to her apartment, Jeremy was already sitting in the parking lot. She got out of the car, extremely pissed by his assertiveness. He had a lot of nerve to show up at her home without officially being invited. Why was he harassing her when he had a pregnant girlfriend he needed to attend to? He slowly got out of his car carrying a huge bouquet of red roses in his right hand.

"Hey, beautiful, you have a hard day at work today?"

"Jeremy, I thought I asked you to call me?"

"I did, but you didn't answer."

"I meant before showing up."

"What? Are you unhappy to see me or something, sweetie?"

Kayla just took a deep breath and headed towards the door of her downstairs apartment. Jeremy followed closely behind without saying another word. She opened the door and turned on the chandelier style light in the living room. He then walked ahead of her and voluntarily gave himself a tour.

"Nice place Hi-C," he said, trying to be funny.

"Yeah, thanks." His so–called humor didn't appease her at all.

"Some beautiful roses for the beautiful lady," he said as he handed them to her and sat down on the couch.

"Oh, how sweet, thanks." She was trying not to sound too repugnant, but she really hated his guts.

"You can go ahead and take your shower if you want to, I'll just watch a show or something and if you want me too, I can come in and wash your back like I use to."

She was trying to decide was he joking or had he seriously lost it. Even if she had manure on herself, she would have sat there in it until he left.

"Jeremy, I'm tired as hell so if there is anything that you feel you want to say, feel free to get it off your chest because I'll be going to bed soon."

"Well, you know about what I told you earlier right?" he began.

Kayla nodded her head in agreement as he continued. "You also know that I've wanted a kid for a while and how I feel about having kids and getting married. The problem is, she's having my baby but…I'm in love with you, so what type of solution can I come up with?"

"Therapy?" She couldn't believe she said that aloud.

"Actually, I was thinking of marrying you and later on convincing her to give us custody." He slowly eased a small box out of his pocket, got down on one knee and asked, "Will you marry me?"

It was right there when Kayla really knew that his mind was gone. She guessed the news of that woman being pregnant and whatever he was going through with his father had caused his normal logic to malfunction.

"For some reason, in your brain you've volunteered me to be a step-mom after you've cheated? Are you nuts?"

At that moment, she realized that he was serious. He had really conjured up a mastermind plan to live happily-ever-after with her and his unborn child. She could see the disappointment and anger in his eyes as he rose from the floor and got directly in her face as if he was purposely trying to intimidate her.

"What else do you think you are going to do, get some thug guy who won't do anything for you and cheat on you? All men cheat, Kayla, at least I take care of home."

"No, I'm going to get a man who isn't going to make me feel like I'm less then him and who doesn't disrespect me by calling me inhumane names."

"Grow up, Kayla, and quit crying. That's your problem now, you too proud with your stuck-up ass."

"But you are sitting here trying to marry me, huh?"

"Girl, please, women come a dime a dozen, I can do better than you."

"Good because that puts this ass back on the market."

It was at that point when he realized she no longer belonged to him. She had gotten her own apartment; she was paying her own bills, and didn't need him for anything. Not even the lousy lunch he tried to take her to earlier.

He suddenly grabbed her by her arms and pulled her in towards his body. He forced kisses on her neck while repeating how sorry he was. The more and more she struggled to pull away, the tighter his grip had gotten.

She was beyond terrified and had never been so helpless in her life. It felt as if some hobo had broken into her home and tried to attack her.

"GET OFF OF ME!" she screamed, hoping the next-door neighbors would hear her.

"I'd kill you if I ever even think you've been with somebody else," he raged as he pushed her against the wall.

She continued to scream but it didn't work. She made a swift move and butted him in the face with her forehead as hard as she could. He let go of his grasp and immediately checked his nose. She attempted to run towards the door as quickly as she could while trying to grab her cell phone from her back pocket. As soon as she got her hand on the doorknob, she felt his forceful hands grab her arm as he pulled her back to where he stood and backhand slapped her to the ground. He grabbed the cell phone and threw it up against the wall, breaking it into pieces. He then dragged her by the arms down the hall towards the bedroom while she attempted to kick wildly, frequently throwing him off his balance. He finally managed to get her in the room and then threw her on the bed and sat on her legs while holding her arms to the side.

"Do you realize how much time and money I put into you? For some reason you think another dude is about to reap the benefits. You're mine forever," he vented as he moved closer up on her torso, pinning her arms down with his knees. He began to pull off his shirt. She couldn't even cry. She was in so much shock and disbelief about what was happening in her very own home. He probably had been planning this entire episode since he found out she had an apartment. She just prayed someone would wake her up from this nightmare. What did she do to deserve such torment? How could a man she has known so long be on top of her about to rape her?

"Kayla, you will never believe what happened," assistant nurse, Rebecca, said as Kayla followed her to a private area. "Destiny is here in the hospital in critical condition."

"What!" Kayla gasped.

"Girl, yes! You know that everyone around here knew she was messing with a married man, so somehow, the wife found out, but that's not the sick part. Supposedly, the wife and the husband ended up tying her up, raping her, and then beating her."

"You're lying!" Kayla exclaimed.

"She is in section B1 of the intensive care unit. You can go see for yourself, and oh, don't tell anyone that I told you," Rebecca said, walking off.

Kayla didn't move. She was trying to process the information in her head. Rebecca had to have been exaggerating, she was known for doing that. Then again, maybe Rebecca was seeing how Kayla would react to the news knowing that Destiny was the one who had gotten her transferred.

Kayla wondered was Rebecca trying to see if she was involved. However, Rebecca couldn't stand Destiny either, since Destiny had slept with her ex-boyfriend, so she knew Rebecca hadn't reformed. She decided to go down to the ICU and see for herself.

Chapter One

"Donna, this wedding reception is nothing short of amazing!" Kelly bragged, one of Donna's coworkers.

"Thank you, girl. You learn to appreciate the finer things in life when your man wants nothing but the best for you. I told you two that this would be a day for everyone to remember."

"Yeah, I must say it's hard to top three fountains of Moët and Gucci watches for the entire wedding party. Now, you just got to make sure he's able to perform since he's almost twenty years your senior," Anthony stated.

144

"Don't mind him...I mean her," Kelly said as she nudged Anthony in the side.

"Oh, you know I'm not. Anthony probably just wants to get laid by my man because he's run out of men to lay at the office."

"You're lucky it's your wedding day and you look too beautiful for me to roast, bitch."

Beautiful was an understatement for the new Mrs. Donna Carter. Her backless dress accentuated her curvaceous hips as the inseams of her white, sequenced gown pulled closely together to showcase her supple breast. Even Beyoncé herself would have been wowed.

"Excuse me...uh...Kelly, if you don't mind I have to steal my wife for a moment." Troy interrupted, gently waltzing his new bride away from them.

"Did he really just act like I wasn't standing here? See, that's why I don't like his ass."

"I'm sure his ass is the only thing you do like," Kelly said as she snickered.

"No, I am not being funny. He is a total homophobic and that's not cool. Before you know it, he'll make her stop hangin' with us. Yes, you too, bitch, while you're looking all sideways at me."

"Did you forget that we all work at the same place?"

"Duh, he'll make her stop working, genius."

"Donna is not that weak-minded to quit her job."

"With all the money he got he can buy her a new job just like he bought his hair plugs."

"Something is seriously wrong with you," Kelly laughed. "Besides, even if she did quit, she wouldn't quit us."

"Well, either way someone needs to teach him a lesson in manners and acceptance."

"Calm down, Anthony. Don't get your panties in a bunch from over thinking. It could have been a simple oversight. He probably just didn't remember you."

"Bitch, no one forgets the queen. And for your info, I'm not wearing any panties."

"You are so nasty."

"Bitch, you don't know the half of it. Now, let's go get some drinks furbished by Mr. Anti-Homely himself."

Donna followed her husband, noticing that he had a tight squeeze on her hand. Observing that he didn't even acknowledge Anthony, this was probably going to be a brief spill about him being there. Donna didn't care. She knew her friends before she even met Troy, so she refused to let him dictate her relationships.

"What is that thing doing here?" Troy asked as they mingled on the dance floor.

"That is very disrespectful. Anthony is my friend," Donna stated, slightly agitated.

"Whatever it is; I told you that I didn't want it at my wedding."

"This isn't the wedding, it's the reception, and since when did you think that you were going to be able to choose my friends?"

"Thy shall not be disobedient to thine husband."

"Exactly. You are my husband, not my father."

"Perhaps someone should have been your father and taught you right from wrong."

"Are you really doing this on our wedding night?"

"Look, I have a business meeting in about an hour and a half. Finish up with your little friends, so we can still make our flight and I can spoil you in the Caribbean." He said, kissing her on the forehead and walking off to greet his daughter who was waving from the other side of the room to get his attention.

Donna hated when Troy would try to start an argument and then throw something extravagant in her face so that she wouldn't press the issue. Donna had expressed to Troy early on in the relationship that her mother and father both died in a car accident when she was seven. She went from foster home to foster home and the journey was beyond horrifying.

Although Troy sometimes had the jerkiest attitude about things, he treated her like a princess. Money wasn't an object since he was the carpeting tycoon of south Arizona. Besides, she was head-over-hills in love with Troy and would do just about anything to please him.

Troy was older and wasn't as physically active as Donna, but his magic stick still did the trick most of the time. The only drawback was that he couldn't last long unless he took Viagra, which ultimately gave him bad migraines.

Donna sometimes found herself pretending during sex, but Troy was the master at giving oral, which compensated for his stamina shortage. For a middle-aged man he was still very handsome and adventurous. He was actually about a ninety percent upgrade from all the other losers she had dated, so his minor flaws were acceptable.

The only other problem that Donna had was that she didn't like how Troy allowed his daughter to treat her. The nerve of her, Donna thought. Who allows their child to not only be absent from the wedding, but to show up at the reception and not speak? Now that Donna was officially moving into Troy's mansion, Monica had no choice but to abide by her rules whenever she came over to visit. She may not ever acknowledge her as her stepmother, but she sure in the hell was going to respect her as one.

"Monica, I'm glad you decided to come. I see you've changed your mind about your stepmother." Troy said, walking over to embrace his daughter Monica.

"Dad, she's not my mother. She's only about six or seven years older than me. Did you tell mom about the marriage?"

"Age is not defined with love, yet love is graced by infinite passion in youth," he said, totally ignoring her question.

"Yeah...sure, dad. I find it very convenient for a young office assistant to marry a rich mogul who technically could be her dad."

"Outside of love, the benefit of a union should go both ways. You would know that if you didn't have that son-of-a-bitch boyfriend leeching off of you."

"Dad, Eric is trying to open up his own fitness center. How is that leeching?"

"When was the last time he bought you something or paid for a date?"

"Dad, this isn't the time to discuss this. Listen, I need you to wire a thousand dollars in my account."

"Have you spoken to Donna yet?" He asked, totally ignoring her request.

"I was gonna-"

"So you have the guts to ask me for money on my wedding day, but you haven't even spoken to my wife?"

"I'm going now, dad. Could you wire the money now? Please and thank you." She added, walking over towards Donna.

"Hi, Donna. I came to say congratulations and you look nice." Monica stated, in the driest tone.

"Oh, is this your way of trying to act decent or did someone offer you some kind of incentive to talk to me."

"You know...whatever, Donna. You think you know everything, but you're no smarter than I am. We could have practically been in the same school together at some point."

"And it just burns you up that I'm the new apple of your daddy's eyes, doesn't it?

"Be careful what you say to me, Donna. You should always remember that I'll always be his daughter."

"That may be true, but now that we're married, I will always have access to the finances. I suggest you play nice. You wouldn't want the rent on your apartment to accidentally get defaulted."

As Monica walked off with a mean glare on her face, Donna knew that dealing with her was going to be challenging. She was the youngest daughter of her husband's two girls, so he had spoiled her rotten. Perhaps, Troy's missing ex-wife played a role in Monica's lack of respect for her.

Donna found it quite strange that she up and left the kids after the divorce. Although they were grown, it would seem as if she would at least stay in contact with her kids. Almost a year had passed and they heard nothing from her.

According to Troy, their mother did send them gifts with no return address for their birthdays and Christmas. Troy claimed that he loaned their mom some money before she left because she wanted to explore the world with her new friend guy. He also told the girls that their mom still randomly calls him from a private number to check on them. Donna just figured that she had a mental breakdown after the divorce and needed time to find herself. As selfish as it was, their mother being gone was one less person she had to deal with when it came to Troy.

"Drive!" Monica demanded to her boyfriend Eric, who was sitting in the car.

"What's your problem?"

"I literally hate that bitch!"

"Babe, that's his wife. You two are gonna have to find a way to get along."

"Not if I can help it."

"Babe, what are you plotting in that big, pretty head of yours?"

"Don't worry about it, Eric Bernard Ferguson."

"Hey! What did I tell you about calling me by my full name," he quickly said, playfully poking her in the neck.

"Stop!" She complained. "You're so annoying."

"And you're too damn sensitive. You need to just stay out of your dad's and Donna's business."

"Shut up and drive. I'm almost tempted to get rid of you just like I'm going to get rid of dirty Donna."

We Were Still Kids (Sample)

Charlie and Joey stood stiff as they looked at Jodie in awe. Joey was young enough to go for it, but Charlie was skeptical. She couldn't believe that Jodie was falling for it, too.

"He's a liar. How would he know our parents?" Charlie asked.

"Well, he asked me who did we stay with, and when I told him Grandma Rose, he said 'yeah, I know your parents. Y'all are those Johnson kids' and I hadn't told him anything," Jodie explained.

"Well, duh, that's my teacher, so I'm sure it wouldn't be hard for him to remember my last name," Charlie said in a matter-of-fact tone.

"Everybody knows he's just a temporary replacement for Ms. Kindle," teased Jodie.

"So?"

"So…what makes you think you're so special that he learned your last name in one day?"

"At least I don't believe everything I hear. You're more gullible than Joey and he's the youngest."

"And you're just mad he told me about mom and not you because he thinks I'm the pretty one," Jodie snapped back.

"Yeah, pretty ugly," Joey said, playfully pushing Jodie's arm and running towards the porch.

As Jodie ran after him towards the house, Charlie's feelings were hurt. Not because of what Jodie said about their looks; Charlie already knew Jodie was prettier than her. Charlie just didn't think that Mr. Frye would like Jodie more than he liked her.

About an hour or so later grandma had arrived home from work. Charlie was sitting in the front room sulking. She tried to hide her feelings, but she clearly wasn't good at it.

"Pick your face up, girl, before somebody step on it," said Grandma Rose as she walked toward the kitchen.

"Yes, grandma," she softly replied.

"What's the matter with you, Charlie?"

Charlie knew she couldn't hide anything from her grandma, but she didn't want to tell her what was bothering her. Charlie figured she'd whip her butt if she told her grandmother she was sad over something silly such as not being favored by a teacher.

"Everything was going fine until I got to homeroom this morning. We got a new teacher, grandma, and I'm not sure if things will work out," she finally said.

"Oh, it'll be okay, Charlie, I'm sure your teacher will like you just as much as the old teacher did. Now, go wash up for dinner."

"Ok, grandma."

Later that evening, Charlie quietly sat down at the dinner table and kept her mouth full, so she didn't have to do a lot of talking. Grandma told the others Charlie was upset because her old teacher was gone, but Jodie knew better. She knew she had crossed the line. Charlie could tell Jodie felt bad from the way she put her head down every time Charlie looked across the table at her.

After dinner, grandma made them clean up and get ready for bed. Joey had to get his hair brushed every night, so his eczema wouldn't flare up on his scalp. This gave Jodie a little time to talk to Charlie alone. She gave Charlie a push as they hopped in the bed.

"Are u still mad at me?" Jodie asked.

"No, who could stay mad at the prettiest girl in the world."

"Come on, really, Charlie? I didn't mean anything by it, besides; you are my sister, so you look just like me."

"I'm flattered," Charlie said, forging a fake smile.

"Come on, are we cool again, or do I have to call u a pretty toad for the rest of the week?"

They both started to laugh. They laughed so hard that grandma yelled to the back, giving them a warning as they scrambled to get in the bed. Feeling better, Charlie lay down and began to daydream about things she wanted to do on summer break.

"I love you, Charlie poop," Jodie said.

"I love you, too, beautiful toad," responded Charlie with a soft giggle and then they were both fast asleep.

It was finally Friday and the kids were happy that the weekend was approaching. Charlie wasn't as enthusiastic about her new teacher as she was the day before. She couldn't help but think he liked Jodie more than he did her. Jodie wasn't smarter than her or as funny as her. Jodie was only prettier than her and not by much. Charlie knew that teachers had their favorites, but good Lord; Jodie wasn't even in Mr. Frye's class. Maybe he just told Jodie about mom because she was older and assumed Jodie would better understand whatever he told her. On the other hand, Charlie knew it didn't matter because whatever he told Jodie about mom, Jodie would tell her.

Once school was over, Charlie went to meet up with Jodie and Joey outside by the school gymnasium. By the time she rounded the corner, she saw one of Joey's teachers standing with them with a big brown bag in her hand.

"Hey Charlie!" Jodie said as she ran up to her. "Guess what?"

"What?"

"Joey won the brown bag special in his class today!"

"What's the brown bag special?"

"It's fresh tomatoes, bell peppers, onions, carrots, and potatoes from Ms. Noel's garden."

Ms. Noel was the fourth-grade science teacher who had a green thumb. She would sporadically bring vegetables and fruits to school and one lucky kid in her class would win the collection in a drawing. Science was the only class Joey liked, so it was no surprise when he won.

Almost as if he had heard his name, Mr. Frye walked around the corner swinging his keys around his finger. Charlie began to wonder was he following them around the school. Why did he just seem to pop up when they were all together? Mr. Frye's humorous persona soon began to turn into annoyance.

"Hey kids. I found out in the teachers' lounge that little Joey won the brown bag surprise. Congratulations, sport!" He said, rubbing Joey's head.

"Yeah, I'm normally always in trouble, but not this time," Joey gleamed.

"Well, I'll be more than happy to give you guys a lift," offered Mr. Frye.

"No, we're taking the bus," blurted Charlie.

"Charlie, that's not polite. Sure, Mr. Frye, just drop us off where you left us the other day."

"Will do, I just have to stop by my house first."

"Jodie, you know grandma ain't about to play with us being late."

"It's fine, Charlie, trust me."

"No, I'm riding the bus," Charlie argued, storming off from them.

"Charlie, wait." Jodie said, catching up with her. "What's the real problem?"

Charlie couldn't admit that she was upset that her teacher seemed to favor her. It wasn't fair that everyone seemed to like Jodie. Joey had his science teacher, and they all had Grandma. Why couldn't Charlie have one person to herself?

"He's just becoming a weirdo and I don't like it."

"Yeah, but don't you wanna know about momma?"

"Yeah, but-"

"Come on, Charlie poop, I got this. We'll be home before grandma even knows anything."

Charlie was skeptical as she allowed Jodie to grab her hand as she followed her older sister. There was an eerie feeling running through Charlie's veins that she just couldn't shake. It didn't take being a psychic for Charlie to sense something was about to go wrong.

The Doctor's Inn: A Private Practice (Sample)

Part II Now Available

"Brad!" she cried. "Stop it, please."

"Let me go!" He demanded.

"You can't do this! You love me!"

Brad flung open the door and shoved her out. He glared at her, his eyes starting to glaze over as tears fought to break out. "I loved you. But I was a fool. I am done being your play toy. Find another sucker to play your game. Goodbye, Jenna."

He stepped back, away from the threshold, and then he slammed the door, shutting out Jenna's lying face. If he could he would shut out his bitter reality. It was a solemn moment for him. If only he could rewind the instance and not had went for her phone at all.

The living room seemed to spin around him, and he felt himself free-falling. Seven years ago, he had thought he found a rose. How was he to know that the beautiful woman was nothing but a thorn in a roses clothing? She continued to slam her hand against the door as she begged him to talk to her. He stood there on the opposite side, almost tempted to open it but he couldn't. He couldn't allow her to make a mockery of him by trying to justify something that was evident.

She finally gave in by telling him she was going to go to her mom's house. She suggested that he needed some time to cool off and rationalize things. He peeked through the window and watched her slowly walk away while calling someone on her cell phone.

Clutching his head as though he would crack it open, he dropped listlessly on a couch. He still couldn't believe what had transpired in a matter of minutes. He then performed an act he had not attempted since his childhood. It was an act he thought he had outgrown. He wept.

www.ingramcontent.com/pod-product-compliance
Lightning Source LLC
Chambersburg PA
CBHW022129170626
46808CB00002B/910